D1528855

MOON OF MADNESS

THE SPANISH BIT SAGA

Books by Don Coldsmith

The Spanish Bit Saga:

Trail of the Spanish Bit
The Elk-Dog Heritage
Follow the Wind
Buffalo Medicine
Man of the Shadows
Daughter of the Eagle
Moon of Thunder
The Sacred Hills
Pale Star
River of Swans
Return to the River
The Medicine Knife
The Flower in the Mountains
Trail from Taos
Song of the Rock

Fort de Chastaigne
Quest for the White Bull
Return of the Spanish
Bride of the Morning Star
Walks in the Sun
Thunderstick
Track of the Bear
Child of the Dead
Bearer of the Pipe
Medicine Hat
The Lost Band
Raven Mocker
The Pipestone Quest
Moon of Madness

The Changing Wind
The Traveler
World of Silence

Rivers West: The Smoky Hill

Runestone
Tallgrass
Southwind
The Journey Home

Horsin' Around
Horsin' Around Again
Still Horsin' Around

MOON OF MADNESS

THE SPANISH BIT SAGA

DON COLDSMITH

GOLDMINDS
NASHVILLE, TENNESSEE

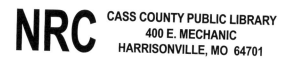

Goldminds Publishing, Inc.
1050 Glenbrook Way, Suite 480
Hendersonville, TN 37075

PUBLISHER'S NOTE

Printed in the United States of America

www.goldmindspub.com

INTRODUCTION

Let me tell you about Don Coldsmith, the author of the book you now hold—*Moon of Madness*, the last installment in the Spanish Bit saga—and a character so colorful he might have come from the pen of Mark Twain, if only Twain had been born a Kansan.

I met Don at the Tallgrass Writing Workshop at Emporia State University in 1987. He was a beloved family doctor who had written a novel published by Doubleday called *Trail of the Spanish Bit*, which became a successful series of books. I had read the first book in the series a few years before, having checked it out of a public library in the southeast corner of the state, and it touched something in me that I immediately recognized as original and uniquely Kansan. Don had taken some well-worn pieces of state folklore, inspired mostly by Coronado's march across the plains in 1541, and woven something new and compelling. What if a young conquistador had been injured and left behind in the heart of an unfamiliar continent, his survival ultimately depending on adoption by the plains Indians he originally despised? Across two dozen books Don told the story of Spaniard Juan Garcia and his descendants and the way in which the introduction of the elk dog—the horse—had changed the fortunes of the tribe Don only described as the People.

Don's genius was in discarding all of the tired conventions of the formula western and telling a story simply, and from the viewpoint of the Native Americans who often had been so marginalized in history and fiction. Eventually, Don gave up medicine to write full-time, and the popularity of the Spanish Bit saga made Don as beloved an author as he had been a country doctor. To date, more than six million copies of the Spanish Bit series are in print.

Don had a natural way with people, supportive and inspiring and demanding all at once. Don became my mentor at that writing workshop in 1987, and he introduced me to his agent, Barbara Puechner, and his editor, Greg Tobin. Soon, Barb was my agent, and eventually Greg became my editor. I became part of an extended family of literary types, more or less associated with the Western Writers of America, of which Don had been president. This sounds pretty straightforward now, but in reality it was a complicated journey in which I made many false starts, suffered disappointments of my own making, and even gave up in despair a couple of times. Don, however, was always on my side. He never gave up on me, and he never let me give up on myself for long.

In his approach to writing, Don was generous and down to earth. When aspiring writers would ask what kind of word processor he used, Don would remove whatever pen he happened to have in his shirt pocket and read them the name of the farm supply store on the barrel. When others complained about not having the time to write, he would patiently explain that he had written *Trail* longhand, on whatever paper he could find, while pulling night shifts at the local hospital—and often while waiting for a baby to be ready to be born. Go anywhere in Emporia and mention his name and typically somebody will say Doc Coldsmith delivered them, or their children.

In addition to being a best-selling author and family physician, Don had also, at various times in his career, been a combat medic in the Pacific; a youth director for the YMCA; a Congregational minister; adjunct professor of English; and a gunsmith, rancher, taxidermist, radio disc jockey, grain inspector, and piccolo player. I never heard him play the piccolo, but I imagine he approached it with the characteristic Coldsmith enthusiasm.

Don was born Feb. 28, 1926, in Iola, Kansas, the son of a Methodist minister. He was a graduate of Baker University and the University of Kansas School of Medicine, and he and his wife, Edna, raised five daughters. For thirty years, he wrote a syndicated column, "Horsing Around." He won the Spur Award for best mass market novel from the Western Writers of America, the Edgar Wolfe Literary Award, and was inducted in to the Writers Hall of Fame. But I'm guessing he was proudest when, in 1993, he was named Distinguished Kansan of the Year.

In 1985, he was among the founders of the Tallgrass Writing Workshop at Emporia State, as a way of giving back, to help foster a community of aspiring western writers. At that third annual workshop, where I met Don, and I remember him telling the story of how he found an old Spanish-style bit in a barrel of odds and ends, and wondering how such an unusual piece of horse tack found its way to Kansas.

"If only that bit could talk," I remember Don saying.

The bit did talk, and Don listened.

Moon of Madness was completed shortly before Don's death on June 25, 2009. He was 83. It was two days before the twenty-fourth annual Tallgrass Writing Workshop. Now, I'm the director of the workshop, which is still held every June on the Emporia State campus, where I'm an associate professor, and my nineteenth novel will be released this summer. I'll never get used to having the workshop without Don, but his spirit survives.

As does his story of the People.

Max McCoy
Emporia
May 1, 2013

FOREWORD

To the People, November is the Moon of Madness. At this season, the days are growing shorter. Leaves are falling. Geese and ducks are following the urge of their heritage... Fly south, far to the south, to warmer climates! Bears feast on nuts and berries, fattening for the coming hibernation. Other creatures begin strange and unusual behavior. The upland birds who do not migrate, often do foolish and even fatal things, flying headlong into the newly-bared limbs of trees which have just dropped their foliage.

It is the rutting season of the deer. The bucks, young and old alike, seem to lose all sense of reason. In their search for romance, they become oblivious to danger, and often place themselves in fatal situations. This, in modern times, translates to thousands of deer fatalities on the highways during November. It is also appropriate to note that among modern humans, November marks a high point in the symptoms of mental illness. Depression falls like a blanket across the land. What if, this year, the fading sun really does go out? We know better, but the nagging doubt remains. The suicide rate comes to an annual peak, along with the occurrence of violent acts toward others.

It is the Moon of Madness.

In the early 1800s, in the territory newly acquired by the United States as the Louisiana Purchase, there occurred a series of massive earthquakes over a period of several months. The New Madrid Fault, named for a small settlement in what would become Missouri, produced more than 200 "moderate to large" earthquake shocks during this period, defined as magnitude 4.3 to 7.7 on the modern Richter scale. More than 1800 shocks of lesser magnitude were reported.

The series of quakes was felt over an area of 210,000 square miles, involving parts of at least seven present-day states. This represents two to three times the area affected by the Alaskan quake in 1964, and more than ten times that of the California quake which destroyed San Francisco in 1906.

There are descriptive eyewitness accounts: Areas of land rising and dropping twenty to thirty feet... Lakes, many miles in length, where there were none before... Waterspouts higher than the tallest trees... It is said that the Mississippi River flowed backward for three days, filling the beds of the newly formed lakes.

In this area of disturbing events, there was a widely dispersed but varied assortment of people. White settlers, possibly Spanish, French, or American, since all three nations had possessed sovereignty there within the past decade. There were natives of several tribes and nations, known to have been in the area or moving through. Trappers, traders, surveyors, explorers. The quakes would not distinguish their victims. How could one decide what to do, when there is no place to run for safety? It would be enough to lead to madness...

CHAPTER ONE

It was the month of June by the calendar of the white man. For the People, the Moon of Roses, when the Great Plains flaunt their beauty.

By tradition, it was the moon in which the various bands of the People gathered each year for the most important of their ceremonies, the Sun Dance. It was a time of reunion for the far-flung bands of the People. The "Elk-Dog People," they were sometimes called. They were among the first to use the horse in the southern plains. The tales of the hair-faced outsider who rode the First Horse the People had ever seen were often retold during the Sun Dance.

"Heads Off," that newcomer had been called, because of a shiny helmet he had been wearing when they first discovered him, injured and bleeding. He removed the metal headgear, and to those watching he had appeared to take off his head.

He had been adopted into the Southern band, and had become a respected teacher as they accepted the benefits of the horse for the hunting of the buffalo. Even now, there were men who proudly wore a fringe of facial hair on the upper lip, to imply the presence of Heads Off in their ancestry. But that was long ago.

The gathering for the Sun Dance was essentially a religious theme, based on the return of the Sun, personalized as Sun Boy. Each season he drove the forces of Cold Maker back to the ice caves in the North during the Moon of Awakening, white man's March.

With Sun's revival came the return of the grass, and in turn the buffalo, the basis of the People's lives. This was a time of worship, for prayers of thanksgiving and supplication, expressions of patriotism, for fulfillment of vows made during the year, and of other vows made anew for the coming season.

The Sun Dance also provided an occasion to visit with relatives and friends in other bands. It was a time of reunion for some, as young people rejoined their own families after a year with a relative. Many a frustrated teenager found that his parents had achieved much wisdom during the season of his absence, while he lived in the lodge of an aunt and uncle in another band. Sometimes the families would "trade" youngsters for a season, with much benefit to all.

But aside from all of this, the ceremonies and the reunions, it was a time for fun. There would be games and contests, horse races and gambling. Wagering would be a prominent feature, associated with the contests and races.

Gambling with the plum stones was a favorite amusement. The yellow seeds of the prairie plum thickets were used for this purpose, after the flesh of the fruit was removed. An odd number of the stones was selected... three, five, or seven, usually. One side of each was painted with a red dot. Each of two gamblers would choose, red or yellow. Then the stones were shaken in a gourd cup, to be tossed or rolled upon a blanket or other smooth surface, much like the dice of the white man. Betting was sometimes heavy. And of course, there were always a few who would wager on anything. Seeing two birds in a distant tree, some would bet on which would be the first to fly.

An important feature of the gathering was always the Big Council. It was assembled only once each year, on this occasion, as soon as the last of the seven far-flung bands arrived. Traditionally, the last arrival would be the Eastern band, whose reputation for foolishness was legend. There were many such stories, usually exaggerated in the telling, and used by the other bands in the education of their children...

"Don't do that! People will think you belong to the Eastern band!"

Or sometimes, a person who has experienced a foolish accident, such as a fall from his horse...

"Well, was not his grandfather of the Eastern band?"

This season was no different. Even the far-away Red Rocks band from the foothills of the mountains to the west had arrived, but there was no sign of the Eastern contingent. Some, concerned for the welfare of relatives in the missing band, began to voice doubts. Others suggested that they proceed with the council. After all, there was a limit to the length of time that the entire nation could meet together. The hundreds of horses, which represented a great part of the wealth of the People, required a great amount of grass. Already the young men who herded them were voicing concern as to whether there would be enough forage for the herds.

The chieftains of the already gathered bands conferred with the Real-chief, elected by the leaders of the People. Should they proceed without the Eastern band? At least, with the Big Council? White Buffalo, the holy man, would set in motion the ritual five days' ceremonies of the Sun Dance after the Council.

He was consulted by the Real-chief, and suggested that a small party of scouts travel a day or two to the east. They could ask some of the Growers who lived in the area whether there was any news of the missing band.

As it happened, the scouting party encountered outriders of the Eastern band, only a day away. One of the scouts would hurry back with the report, while the other two rode with the travelers.

It had been a very unusual year, the Eastern outriders reported.

This brought chuckles and jibes from the other scouts. "Is not every year unusual in the Eastern band?" asked Spotted Dog.

This joking remark was met with dour faces by those from the Eastern band. Usually, they tolerated the teasing with good humor. There was something different here...

"You were not there!" stated one of the outriders peevishly.

"That is true," admitted Spotted Dog, who had spoken before.

This appeared to be serious. "You had many problems?"

"You will hear at the Council!"

This was most unlike the Eastern band. Usually, they made jokes, even about their misfortunes. To refrain from talk about it was definitely not characteristic.

They rode in silence for a little while, heading on toward the site of the Sun Dance. It was a strained silence, and finally the older of the Eastern riders spoke.

The raw challenging tone had softened somewhat.

"There were very bad times," he said. "The earth shook for a long time."

"Yes, a trader mentioned that to someone in the Forest band, it was said."

The Eastern rider gave a sidelong glance, loaded with indignation.

"You have no idea!" he snapped.

"Then, tell us about it!"

"You will hear, when the time comes."

"But I don't understand, friend. It must have been bad... You were injured?"

The other man sighed, and shook his head.

"No, not I... One of our young men... You remember Badger?"

"Maybe... Short, about this high?"

"Yes, that's the one. The story is his. He was not with the band at the time."

Spotted Dog waited for more information, but none was offered. Finally he spoke. "Then, the bad happenings were to Badger, not to the whole band?"

"Maybe so. Badger had the worst. He went mad."

"*Aiee!* He is so, now?"

"Some have said so."

Spotted Dog said nothing for a little while. A thought flitted through his head, that there were probably those who would consider that to lose his mind would be nothing new to Badger. He longed to ask "How could they tell?" but managed to stifle the urge.

Badger was a jokester, one of those who seem dedicated to the principle that something funny can be found in any situation. Rarely, if at all, was he serious. He seemed to revel in the reputation of the Eastern band as foolish people. If an incident had no foolish side, Badger would find one or create it. He was a thorn in the flesh of the more serious elders of the Eastern band. There was a running joke that Badger had given the Eastern band a bad name for foolishness. The standard observation on this was a solemn question: "How can this be?"

They rode in silence a little longer, and finally the Eastern rider spoke again.

"You know that it is bad," he observed, "if Badger has lost his foolishness."

Moon of Madness

CHAPTER TWO

The Eastern band joined the gathering toward dark the next day. It was quickly announced that the Big Council would be held on the following evening. This would allow the Eastern band time to set up their lodges and settle in.

Rumors flew. The Eastern band had obviously had some terrifying experiences. So serious, in fact, that they hardly responded to foolish-people jokes. It seemed inappropriate under the circumstances. The intervening day, waiting for the Council, took on a somber mood. None of the Eastern band had much to say, which seemed a miracle in itself. The others gained the impression that for the entire Eastern band, the earth trembled and shook for a long time. There was, however, the general idea that the young man, Badger, had suffered experiences much more serious than anyone else. This, too, was odd, because one would think that such a well-known clown, famous for his foolishness, would never take anything very seriously. Ah, well, when the time came, maybe they would learn of his experiences.

Meanwhile, questions directed to other young men of the Eastern band were avoided or pushed aside.

"I don't know... I was not there, in that part. Yes, the earth shook some, but talk to Badger. He was there."

"But... Where? And, we cannot talk to Badger. He stays in his parents' lodge."

"Yes, that is true."

The young man in question had been seen only briefly as the family erected their lodge. It was nearly dark, and the People had assumed that once the late-comers had made camp, everyone would begin visiting as always. To some extent, they did, but the uneasy, fearful attitude on the part of the Eastern band cast a shadow over the entire camp.

Goose Feather, chieftain of the Eastern Band, was seen to spend much time in the lodge of the Real-chief, Black Horse, of the Northern band. Such pre-council conferences were expected, since the Real-chief, presiding over the council, must be aware, to some extent, of the experiences of all the bands during the past season. Some reports would be short, with no serious problems. Others of the bands might have been faced with events that could affect the entire Elk-dog nation.

It was with a great deal of interest then, that the entire camp noted the extra time spent by Goose Feather in the lodge of the Real-chief. This, especially since Goose Feather himself had always been a jolly, easy-going leader, appropriate to the Eastern band. It was difficult to imagine him in serious council.

As evening approached, the People began to gather earlier than usual. The arrangement of seating of the chiefs had been prescribed many lifetimes ago. Their circle, closest to the council fire, was largely determined by the direction of the summer range of each band. There had even been an empty seat in recognition of the Lost Band, missing for many generations. Now, that seat had been occupied again, as descendants of that ancient massacre had returned, only a generation ago. Behind each chieftain sat the most honored and respected leaders of his band, and behind them, the families of the rest of the People, each band in a wedge-shaped configuration.

In the present circumstance, with an exciting council expected, there was an effort to arrive early to be assured of a good seat. The chiefs, of course, would traditionally arrive last, as befitting their rank, with the Real-chief arriving last of all, to convene the Council.

Young men of the various bands had searched the prairie for dead trees, usually cottonwoods, and dragged the fuel to the area where the Big Council would occur.

Sun Boy had painted himself with brilliant colors and now slipped below the horizon. Sparks from the council fire fluttered skyward like fireflies, to fade among the stars now appearing one by one. The chieftains, fully aware of each others' approach, now began to thread their way through the crowd, accompanied by a trusted sub-chief or two... Perhaps a holy man or other dignitary of that particular band. Many wore ceremonial paint.

Black Horse, flanked by the holy man, White Buffalo, made his way to the position of the Northern Band's seating, and the two seated themselves. The crowd began to quiet, as Black Horse's pipe bearer filled the ceremonial pipe and handed it to his chief. Then he stepped quickly to fetch a burning twig with which the Real-chief would start the ceremony, by the lighting of his pipe.

Black Horse accepted the twig and ignited the tobacco, blowing a puff of smoke to each of the four winds, then to earth and sky. He then handed the pipe to the man on his left, Goose Feather of the Eastern band. Goose Feather repeated the ceremony, and handed it on, to the chief of the next, the New band. Though they had camped with the People for many generations now, they would always be the "newcomers."

The pipe proceeded around the circle of chieftains, each repeating in turn the homage to the four winds, earth, and sky.

At completion of the circle, Black Horse ceremonially knocked the dottle from his pipe into his palm, and tossed it into the fire. He handed the instrument to the pipe bearer, who cased it carefully and took his seat behind his chief.

The crowd grew tense. Now would begin the narration of the experiences of each band. By tradition, the sequence followed that of the pipe, each chieftain following the one on his right. Through long tradition, the first to be called upon would be the Eastern band, sitting to the left of the Real-chief. There was a murmur of anticipation, and Black Horse raised a hand to quiet the crowd, then turned and nodded to Goose Feather, who stood to speak.

"I am Goose Feather of the Eastern band," he began formally, though everyone was well aware of that fact. "We have had a very dreadful season. I am made to think that all of us are fortunate to be alive. Yet, with all of it, we lost not a single life."

There was a chuckle or two in the back rows of the other bands. It was difficult for some to take the Eastern band seriously. Surely, there must be a joke, such as the time long ago when the Eastern band had camped next to a traditional enemy by mistake. The enemy, taking pity on their ignorance, did not even bother to kill them.

At least, so the story said.

A sharp look from Black Horse quieted the interruption, and the Real-chief nodded to Goose Feather to continue.

"The Eastern band," their chief continued, "had decided to move a little farther south than usual. We met a trader who told us of other tribes moving around, partly because of the coming of more whites. It seemed good to us to see new country. This was not a good thing. You have heard, I am certain, of some of our problems. The earth trembled for a long time, and there was no place to go."

The Real-chief broke tradition for a moment to assist in clarifying the story.

"Goose Feather has told me of this," he interrupted. "How long did this trembling go on?"

"*Aiee*, for many moons!" said Goose Feather. "It is very hard, to even tell of it."

There was a gasp of disbelief. Many moons? A mild trembling of the earth was not unheard of, but no one present, even those who had experienced such an event, had felt it for longer than a few heartbeats.

"This began," Goose Feather went on, "near the end of the Moon of Madness, and went on and on. None of our Eastern band had ever heard of such things. How long could the Moon of Madness last?"

Now there was dead silence. There were no longer any chuckles in the rear.

"This continued through the Moon of Long Nights, and the Moon of Snows," the chief went on. "Yes, the Moon of Hunger, too. It seemed never to stop until the Moon of Awakening."

"Five Moons of Madness?" said someone incredulously.

He was quieted by a stern look from the Real-chief. "It is true!" Goose Feather protested solemnly. "And, you must know... The Eastern band was not even close to the worst of it. That was much farther east."

"Then, how do you know this?" someone asked.

"Stop!" demanded the Real-chief.

The Council appeared to be falling apart, but Black Horse recovered control quickly.

"Let us go no further," he said sternly, "until it is understood that this is the Big Council. It will not be ignored."

The crowd quieted, and the Real-chief spoke again.

"Now," he said soberly, "Goose Feather and I have talked much. This is an important season, especially to our brothers of the Eastern band. Goose Feather has told me of one of their young men who was caught up in the anger of the earth as it tried to shake itself, as a dog shakes water from its fur. That young man, Badger, was caught in the worst of this time of madness. Badger is much better now, it is said, but only now is beginning to talk of his experience."

He paused, and turned to Goose Feather.

"This is true?" he inquired. "Badger is willing to talk of it now?"

"I am made to think so, my chief. He has told Talking Trees, our holy man, some of the things he saw."

"Is Badger here?"

"In the lodge of his parents," answered Winter Wind. "I am his father. He will come if we ask him."

"Can someone go and learn whether Badger will come?" inquired the Real-chief.

"May I suggest," said Goose Feather, "the Big Council could continue while we ask about Badger."

"It is good!" agreed the Real-chief. "Let it be so. Next, the New band?"

The chieftain of the New band related that they had been aware of the earth's shuddering, but had not been closely involved. The same was true of the Forest band, who had had a good season. By this time, however, few of the People were really listening. The big news of the entire Sun Dance this season would revolve around whatever it was that had happened to Badger, of the Eastern band.

After the unusual opening of the Council, with the big news of the season centering on the Eastern band, the reports from the other chieftains seemed flat and lifeless.

There was much curiosity about the experiences of the young man, Badger. Everyone wanted to hear, yet there was a reluctance to intrude on the privacy of someone who had obviously been in close contact with unknown and possibly dangerous spirits, completely foreign to the People.

The Red Rocks band related that they had met and traded with some of the Growers to the southwest of their usual area, with satisfactory results. In a normal year, that would have been a newsworthy event, but now it was eclipsed by the mysterious events to the east.

After the last of the reports, that of the Mountain band, Black Horse spoke to the Council, and those assembled. At this time it was usually announced that the countdown to the Sun Dance would begin.

It was the holy man, White Buffalo, who was charged with the announcement. On each of the next three mornings, in his full regalia and ceremonial paint, the priest would circle the camp, singing his announcement of the coming event. Meanwhile, the family of the Real-chief would be hunting. Their goal was to find the largest and finest buffalo bull available. The head and skin would be used to create an effigy representing the buffalo for the Sun Dance. The arena would be roofed with brush, to provide shade for the dancers and participants during the days of the Dance.

But this time it was not the holy man who spoke to the Council, but the Real-chief.

"I have talked with our holy man," he began. "We are made to think that the time has not come, for the Sun Dance."

There was a murmur from the crowd, and the chief held up a hand for silence.

"It is this thing of the trembling earth, and the Moon of Madness," he explained. "We have talked, White Buffalo and I. We are both made to think that it would be foolish to go ahead with the Sun Dance without learning all we can. Maybe the spirits of the Sun Dance would not mingle well with those of the trembling earth. But how do we learn of this? It is believed by both of us, White Buffalo and I, that we should hear all we can from those who were nearest to the happenings. That one is our brother in the Eastern band, Badger."

There was a muffled gasp from the crowd. Few had even seen the young man in question. There were rumors that he had been stricken with loss of speech. At best, he had always been considered a foolish young man, even by Eastern band standards.

"We have talked with Badger," the chief went on. "His is a powerful story. At first he did not think that he could speak of it, but with the help of our holy man, Badger has come to believe that his story can be told."

A rustle of disturbance flowed through the crowd and settled back as Black Horse raised his hand to silence it. "Badger has agreed to speak to us," he went on. "His story is long... White buffalo and I have heard only part of it. This will not be easy for Badger. So, since it now grows late, we will have the story fire tomorrow at dark, when our young brother will tell us of his experience. For now, the Council is adjourned."

Excitement built through all of the next day, and people began to gather long before Sun Boy performed his evening ritual. There was tension in the air. Some families brought food, and proceeded to eat during the long wait until the fire was lighted.

Since this was an unusual situation, not a council but a story fire, there was no formal pipe ceremony. The crowd gathered, restlessly looking toward the Eastern band's camp area, waiting.

Eventually, of course, Badger was seen, threading his way among the lodges, flanked by his parents. They had no other child, and Badger had been their pride and joy. This, thought many of the People, was the cause of at least part of Badger's immaturity and silliness. There was much questioning as to whether this young man could be serious enough, for long enough, to tell a straight story.

To the onlookers, the young man appeared different, somehow. He seemed taller, or at least carried himself in a more dignified manner. And, despite the rumors that he had been on the verge of madness, there was a new sense of growing confidence in his demeanor.

The trio made their way to the place where the speaker was to stand. They paid their respects to the Real-chief, and the parents stepped away, to find seats. Their pride in their son was apparent, but there was also a look of concern.

Badger seemed far more confident than many had expected, as he nodded to the nearby leaders of the assembled bands. Possibly the responsibility that now fell upon him had made him grow to the occasion. He was tense and nervous, yes. But the young man who stood before them was not the silly child that many remembered.

Here was a man. There was a look of experience, of pain and sorrow. There was, in the dark, deep-set eyes, a reflection of things not often seen by mere mortals. Yet there was a confidence, a wisdom acquired possibly at great expense.

The crowd quieted, and he began to speak. The confidence in his face came through in a deeper, more mature voice than many of the onlookers had expected.

Here was a man whose demeanor, though humble, commanded respect, and the crowd was ready for his words.

CHAPTER THREE

I am called Badger, son of Winter Wind and Crow Woman, of the Eastern band. I have been asked to tell of the things that happened to me and the things I saw during the past season, since the People last met for the Sun Dance. This is hard for me to tell, because it was a time of madness. The Moon of Madness seemed to go on and on. But... No, let me begin at the beginning.

Last season's Sun Dance was held near Medicine Rock, you remember. As the bands parted to travel, each in its own direction, I must have been an embarrassment to my parents. I was certain that I knew everything there was to know. I am their only child, and the family has no close relatives. Most of the young men of the People have the benefit of an uncle to teach them. Usually, the brother of his mother, no? But, my mother is from another tribe, with no family among the People.

Of course, I grew up in the Rabbit Society, with the other boys and girls. We were taught the Rabbit Dance by the "uncles," and the games that help a child learn to do useful things. We heard the stories of the Trickster and of... What?

Oh, yes, forgive me. I will move along. I was trying to apologize, maybe, for my youth and ignorance. Does not everyone reach a time when parents know nothing at all? I had some friends, equally ignorant, of course. Yet, they had an advantage; each had an uncle or teacher of some sort. My friend Spotted Dog, there, was to spend a year with the Southern band, in the lodge of his mother's sister. Greetings, Dog, we will talk later.

But I had no one to demonstrate to me my ignorance, but my parents. My mother is a fine woman, except that she cannot see any flaw in me, her only child. My father probably did see flaws, but at the time, I could not recognize the value of anything he said. Being a parent, he knew nothing. At least, nothing with any meaning. I am pleased to say that he has learned much since then.

Now, with all of the newly-acquired maturity and wisdom that I had a year ago, I was restless. I considered a vision quest. My father told me that I was not ready yet which, of course, made me all the more certain that I was.

I have since told him that he was right.

Along with all of this, I was burdened with another thing that must be outgrown somewhere along the trail. A young man has the firm belief that he is immortal. Yes, we have seen, all our lives, that people die. There are dangers in the hunt, there are accidents and sickness and old age. A friend of mine was killed when the horse he was riding fell and rolled on him. But a youth does not understand, yet. I knew these things but they had nothing to do with me. Such things only happen to other people.

So, as you see, I was quite unprepared to make decisions of any sort, when such a decision was forced upon me. Or, so I thought.

Our Eastern band left the Sun Dance and traveled back toward our own country. We left the Tallgrass Hills and traveled eastward, across the River of Swans and into the traditional country of the Eastern band. For some reason, probably one that I paid no attention, Goose Feather and our sub-chiefs led the band farther to the south than usual. It was interesting; new things to see, different trees and plants, some animals and birds... Well, new country.

We encountered different people, Growers who live in permanent lodges, and don't move around. Yes, much like the Kenzas, I am made to think. We camped in an area of mixed tallgrass and forest.

One of my friends, Stone Lizard, departed on a vision quest, and I thought to do so, also. My father talked against it, and we were angered at each other, and my mother cried.

By chance, a trader passed through and stopped for a few days at the camp of the Eastern band. He and his wife had a daughter of about my age, maybe a year younger, who was the most beautiful girl I had ever seen. She was bright and funny and friendly, and I fell instantly in love. I was made to think that the girl felt the same.

"White Plume," she was called, and the name seemed to fit. There comes to mind words like "soft" and "warm." She was tall and slender, graceful as a willow tree in a warm breeze, but with all the curves and suggestive bulges where they should be. Her eyes spoke more than words, and her smile could lighten the darkest glade in the forest. She would take my hand and we would walk together, and feel the warmth of each other's presence. Her laugh was like the ripple of... Yes, yes, I'll go on.

Well, she was beautiful. I had been frustrated for two or three seasons, about the coming of age in the girls I knew in the Rabbit Society. There had been those among them who had been my friends. We had competed in the learning of the use of weapons, in racing and riding, swimming, all the things taught to both boys and girls.

Then, a puzzling thing. Their shapes began to change. The buckskin dress was tighter across the chest than before, and appeared softer. At the same time the muscles in their legs below the knee seemed to swell a little, and their hips became... Well, not wider, exactly, but more interesting, somehow. Their personalities changed, and they were more self-conscious about physical contact. No more wrestling! Yes, you laugh, but you know of what I speak!

What was hurtful, though, was that they had begun to forget those of us who had been friends since we were small together. They were far more interested in the young men a year or two older than we were, those their own age. I had not yet realized that the girls begin the changes to maturity somewhat earlier than the boys. Yes, boys see and admire and desire, before they are physically ready to act on these desires. The females, now becoming women, are noticed by young men a year or two older, who are ready to begin courtship. This is hurtful to all young men, to see the female friends of our youth taken from us by men with whom we cannot compete until a year or two later.

Of course, there is possibly a reason for this. The older and stronger men can better provide for support and protection of the mothers of the People's next generation. We, in turn, will begin to sprout face-hair and bigger muscles, and will be looking at the development of the next crop of young women.

But at the time we speak of, I had barely begun to try to pluck the fine hair along my upper lip with the clam-shell tweezers. *Aiee*, that is uncomfortable! But... Yes, yes, I'll move along. I am only trying to explain my reasons for feeling as I have felt. It is those feelings and desires that have a heavy effect on my story. So, bear with me, my friends.

Now, due to my attraction to the young woman, White Plume, I was made to feel a need to appear interested in the activities of her father. I hung around the trader's display, and when he was not occupied in the bartering that must occur in his profession, I would ask him questions. "What is this?"

"This" was a dark lump of a waxy substance, about the size of my fist. I had thought that it might be used to wax sewing sinew. Or, to seal the binding on the point of an arrow, fastening the stone arrowhead to the wooden shaft. Looking back, I am certain that the trader was not fooled for a moment about my motives. He had seen my sidelong glances at his beautiful daughter. But he was a wise man. As long as I professed an interest in his trade goods, he knew where I was, and he could watch me. To watch a potential suitor, of course, was an easy way to make certain that at least one was not overstepping appropriate boundaries of custom and decency. So, as long as I asked questions, I was tolerated. I was foolish enough to think he did not know my real purpose.

The dark waxy lump, he explained, was not intended to fasten arrow points or wax sewing thread. It was, in fact, a substance which could be shaved from the lump into hot water, to make a bitter but not unpleasant drink. It was grown by people far to the south, a substance called chokalatl, he said.

"What is its purpose?" I asked him. "Medicine?" The trader was very vague about that, hinting at secret medicinal uses. I later learned that chokalatl is thought to stimulate sexual desire in women. As I look back, the trader was very tolerant of an ignorant young man who plainly had designs on his daughter. But he was wise. If he had tried to chase me away, I would still have been attracted to his daughter, but would have been more sneaky about it. If he kept me close to him, he could watch me more easily.

I did not realize all of this at the time, of course. I only tried to maintain close contact with him and his family to remain near the girl, White Plume. In this, I was aided considerably by the girl. I am made to think that she was as eager as I was to become better acquainted.

What? You ask more about the chokalatl? I wanted to know more, too! I asked more... How did the trader happen to have it? No, this is becoming more important than I intended. No, it has little to do with my story. I only mention it to show that a trader knows much about many places, many customs, and must trade whatever he can for whatever there is to trade. This is the life of a trader and his family, no? In this way, we have foods, weapons, knives, powder and lead for the thundersticks, the guns themselves, fire-strikers of steel, blankets, many of the things we use.

Aiee, Dog, forget the chokalatl. I don't know what he traded for it. It tasted bitter, a little bit. That's all I can tell you about it. Now, let me go on!

I became close to the family of the trader during the few days they camped with the People. Both of White Plume's parents were good to me, for the reasons I have mentioned. White Plume had a younger brother, who was of an age to be a complete nuisance. Though his given name was Little Buffalo, to many people of the tribe, especially the other boys near his age, he was called Toad. I could happily have done without him. This prevented entirely any intimate moments that might have been significant in the acquaintance... Yes, more than acquaintance.

But, a real friendship was growing between White Plume and me, or so I thought. I began to dread the time when our trails would part, and the trader's family separated from our Eastern band of the People. I suppose that for a time, I was pretending that if I did not allow myself to think about it, the parting would never take place. Stupid, of course, but no one has ever accused a young man in love of possessing good judgment. As the saying goes, "You can always tell a man in love, but you can't tell him much." Is it not so?

But, let me get back to my story. There is much to tell...

Again, remember that I was very young and foolish at the time. At that age, most young people are, but I admit, I was probably worse than most. I need not convince any who knew me of that. Yes, you laugh, I see. So be it. There is much that has happened since that time.

The day came when White Plume came to me with sadness in her face, and told me that her father was ready to leave the camp of the People. Two days, she said.

Ah, I was crushed by the news. I had just begun to feel that our companionship was becoming comfortable. There flashed through my mind that White Plume may have only been teasing me, using me for a temporary companion to avoid the boredom of staying in a community of strangers. In a wave of frustration and anger, I accused her of this.

She cried. I had hurt her with my childish act of temper. *Aiee*, how stupid can a young man be? Quite stupid, as you will soon see. I had convinced myself that I had actually been helpful to White Plume's father, Lone Fox. Well, I carried some packs for him sometimes. It was not entirely questions and sidelong exchange of glances with his daughter. I tried to be useful.

I lay awake a long time that night, feeling that the world had sunk from under me, and I was floundering. What could I do?

I considered asking Fox if I could join him and his family as his assistant. "I'll work hard," I would tell him. But that sounded stupid, even to me. I would have to have a better plan. Ah, you begin to see...

"Father," I said, "I am made to think that it is time for my vision quest."

Yes, we were in unfamiliar territory, where there were unknown people, some of whom might be quite dangerous and even traditional enemies, as far as I knew.

My father was quite calm about it, at least on the surface. At first, that is. We had discussed the vision quest before, but he had easily talked me out of it. He tried to do so this time, but my childish temper intervened, and we were to part in anger. I was very disrespectful, reminding him that the vision quest decision was mine. My mother cried, and begged me to reconsider, but I was angered by this time and would not listen.

I had no intention of undertaking a vision quest, you see. That was only a distraction. My true purpose was to follow the trader and his family, and in a day or two surprise them by walking into their camp and offering to help, as I had been doing in the recent past. It did not occur to me that Lone Fox might not need or want me, or that by the time I rejoined their family, White Plume might have found another playmate.

CHAPTER FOUR

You might say of me that I was behaving very poorly and thoughtlessly, and you would be right. I was like a small child, jumping boldly into a stream, unable to swim, and with no knowledge of the depth.

I knew that the trader and his family were only a day ahead of me. I must catch up quickly, though. Unlike the trails in our Tallgrass Hills, the woodland trails twist and turn. They cross each other, and it would be easy to lose the party ahead if they had turned aside at a fork in the trail.

But I had one advantage. Fox and his family were held to a slower pace by their pack horses. A rider can cover much more distance, at a trot or a canter part of the time, while the pack animals can only walk.

I had not overtaken them by sundown of my first day's travel, which puzzled me a little. I had expected to find them. I chose my camp site and built my fire, keeping it small. I had nothing to cook anyway, carrying some dried meat for the journey. The weather was warm. The fire was mostly for reassurance, and for the purpose of adding a pinch of tobacco to appease the spirits. This lets them know "Here I intend to camp," of course, as the fragrant smoke rises and disappears.

I learned much about campfires since we parted a year ago. It was called to my attention later that white men build a big fire, and must stay farther away from it, sometimes finding it hard to warm themselves. Our people build a small fire and hover close to it, with a better warming.

What? Of course! This is part of my story. Let me tell it!

As I was about to say when I was interrupted, I was settling in for the night, chewing on a piece of jerky as the sky darkened. I picketed my mare, and unrolled my blanket, to sit or lie on, when the horse suddenly lifted her head and whinnied loudly, as if calling to a companion. Instantly, there was a faint answer, from beyond the next hill.

I have never understood how horses do that. To recognize that there is another horse in the area, I mean. They might suspect it, but how do they know when to call out? And, are they not always right about it? Of course! Maybe their hearing is better, but I am made to think it is more than that. A thing of the spirit, maybe.

In this case, I was concerned because I was in unfamiliar country. There was a moment of panic while I scrambled into the shelter of some bushes near by. Then, I began to think about the situation. I must find out where the other horse was, and whether it was wandering loose, or was ridden. More importantly, by whom.

Of course, if there was a war party, they would have muzzled their animals. But, in the dark, in unknown country, I was not thinking of such things. I had much to learn, you see. I still do, I now admit.

I watched and listened, and nothing happened. I began to feel a little foolish. Maybe the voice of the other horse was only an echo... But no, it had seemed real. I decided to go and see.

I muzzled my mare, tying a thong around her nose and lower jaw. She could not graze, of course, but could wait until I had found the source of the other animal's call.

The moon was rising, a day past full, and it would soon provide enough light to be a help. I decided to wait a little while, rather than bump into trees in the dark. You see, I was beginning to gain a little wisdom already. I had a long way to go, in that matter. I still do, but at least I was beginning to learn that we never stop learning.

When I had enough light from the rising moon, I moved on. I was still following the beaten path, stopping for a few heartbeats occasionally to listen ahead. It was not long until I saw the glow of a campfire through the trees. I watched for a little while, but saw nothing except for the flickering light. I was preparing to move on, when there was a rush from behind me and I was thrown to the ground, hard. The breath was knocked from my lungs, and a man was sitting on my back. My face and chest were pressed against the ground, and my attacker had a fistful of my hair, pulling my head back. Something sharp was pressing against the right side of my throat.

I yelled out in terror. For a moment, I thought I was as good as dead. The man could have easily cut my throat.

"No, no!" I screamed. "I meant no harm. Don't kill me!"

I was yelling in our own tongue, of course. I knew no other. It had not even occurred to me that it was unlikely that my attacker would know our language. I could have used hand signs, except that I was pinned to the ground, on my belly, and that it was dark.

"Badger?" asked the voice of the man who sat on me. "Badger?"

It was only a few heartbeats until I realized that my attacker was speaking the language of the People, my own, and that he knew my name.

"What are you doing here?" he asked, still making no effort to remove himself from my back.

Now, I recognized that voice.

"Fox?" I gasped. "Lone Fox?"

"Badger, you should not be here!" he said flatly. "Do your parents know where you are?"

"Of course!" I almost yelled at him. "I am on my vision quest!"

I was truly embarrassed by my own stupidity and how clumsy I had proved to be.

Fox removed his weight from my back.

"A strange place for a vision quest!" the trader grunted as he stood up. "It was your horse that called out?"

"I heard yours, too!" I snapped back at him.

"Of course," he agreed, making me feel all the more foolish.

Finally, my own embarrassment caused me to go on. "I followed you," I admitted. "I wanted to be of help to you, and to learn your trade."

It was only partly true, of course. I knew that he knew, and that he probably suspected the rest, that I was smitten by the loveliness of his daughter.

Many men would probably have cut my throat, taken my horse, and kept moving, under these circumstances. Looking back, I cannot thank Lone Fox enough for the way he treated me, with kindness and understanding.

"I suppose," he said, "that your vision quest is over?"

There was only a hint of sarcasm in his voice.

"I... I will have to start it over," I admitted.

"Then, shall we go to bring your horse? Where are you camped?"

"Not far. I... I'll go to get my things."

I was totally embarrassed now. I was wondering how he would relate my story to his family. Would I even be able to face the object of my affection? Now I began to worry that White Plume might have had far more experience than I suspected. Maybe she had left disappointed suitors all over the plains, and was laughing at them as she moved on. Laughing at me, too?

I considered, as I retraced the trail back to my camp to recover my horse, the possibility that I could simply head on back to the People. But, my pride would not allow it. I would sacrifice a bit of pride, of course, by joining the trader, but after all, had that not been my original plan? And, Fox had not forbidden it. I decided to accept that as a good sign.

Before the moon was half way up the night sky, I was back to the camp of the trader, with my horse, blanket roll, and my few possessions. Fox had built their fire up enough to light my way. I did not know what he might have told his family, but any embarrassment over that was quickly cut short by the smile of his daughter when I entered the circle of firelight. Either she was sincerely happy to see me, or was the best pretender in the world. At that time I did not yet know which, but it was a risk worth taking. Or, so I thought. I was still taking myself far too seriously. But, enough about that. You will see!

Moon of Madness

CHAPTER FIVE

I don't know what might have happened to me if Lone Fox and Dove, his wife, had been other than the caring and thoughtful people that they were. It is embarrassing, to look back now. But, I have already said that, in apology to them, to my parents, and to the People.

It is here that the story of the Madness really begins. Even so, there was a time at first when the world seemed to be moving naturally. It was a summer that passed quickly, because I was working hard. Maybe Fox had decided to test me. If I could become a man worthy of his daughter's bed, he would make me prove it. We never talked of this. It is my own interpretation, but I am made to think it true.

He worked me so hard that I would have scarcely had the strength to get into trouble with his daughter. There were always packs to handle. I quickly learned to balance the loads on each side of the pack saddle, and the knots and hitches to use. Fox had two pack horses and a mule, the first I had ever seen. Its sire is a donkey, and its mother a mare. It has a strange spirit, unfamiliar to me, yet I came to love it, later.

I shudder to think of what might have happened if White Plume had, at that time, rejected me. I could not have stayed with the family, and it is questionable whether I could have survived alone. I had confidence in my ability, of course. I could hunt, as well as any, but I had no knowledge of the area, or of any of the tribes I might encounter, or whether they would be friends or enemies. Nearly all of the other tribes I had seen until that time were either buffalo hunters, like the People, or Growers, like the Kenza or Wichita, who also hunted buffalo. I could talk with them in hand signs. They were different from the People, but not totally unfamiliar.

I had encountered a few white men, whose ways are truly strange. Did you know that their god only visits them four times each moon? It is true, I am told! They call it Sun Day. Maybe they only look for God on that day, which seems strange to us. Most of the whites that the People see on the prairie are trappers and traders, and follow our ways. Some are tribal members, and have wives and families, among the People or our allies, as you know.

I was to meet people, white and red, with far different ways, in the next few moons. Miss-our-ees, Osage, even Cherokees, from far to the East.

But for now, I was learning much about the life of a trader. Sometimes, too rarely, it seemed, there would be a short interval which I could spend with White Plume. It was also fortunate that she responded to my friendship. If she had not, I would have had to leave. It was too close, and too much like being a part of the trader's family. I wonder sometimes yet, how such a situation could have happened, much less have survived for any time at all.

I am not certain, as I look back, whether the presence of White Plume's younger brother helped or threatened our relationship. Little Buffalo, or Toad, was at a most obnoxious age, maybe ten or eleven summers. His mother, of course, adored him, though I could not understand how. It is so with mothers, I have learned. No matter how ugly, how careless, how irresponsible a young man may appear to everyone else, to his mother he can do no wrong. If it seems so, that he did, it must be a misunderstanding of some sort, and she will find an excuse for him. Yes, I see some of you chuckling... This applies to my mother, too, and to my own poor judgment.

But, back to White Plume's brother, Toad. I am sure that his mother resented this name. For quite some time I did not know the child-name, Little Buffalo, that had been given at his formal naming ceremony. I am not certain about how his people might handle that custom. I was made to think, though, that at that awkward age, most tribes use some temporary child-name, until on reaching manhood, a man earns his name. That happens only when it is time for it to be so.

This name of Toad was given to him because of his looks. He had a mouth, drawn down in a perpetual sneer, even when he laughed. When he spoke, or in any situation involving other people, he would open his eyes wide and bug them out, somehow. Well, like those of a toad. I could almost imagine him snapping at flies.

Toad seemed to feel that his duty in life was to make his sister miserable. Yes, I see some nods. Some of you have had such younger brothers. I wondered, even, at one time, if Fox, as a wise father, might have given Toad the duty of interfering with any chance White Plume might have for a romance or a husband.

Considering, though, Toad's whole approach to the world, I doubt that he would have cooperated with anyone, even his father, in such a scheme. In any plan, for that matter. If the boy suspected that some desired or even useful result would occur, he would reject it. That was the kind of child that Toad appeared to be. His mother sometimes scolded him, but very gently.

It was only a day or two after I joined the trader's family when I happened to see an incident that will show how the boy's thoughts worked. I tell it now, because it did become of importance later.

I had been gathering some wood for Dove's cooking fire. We were camped in a wooded area, which always made me a little uneasy. The People live in more open country, usually, where we can stretch our eyes. To be surrounded by trees and brush causes me to feel trapped. Much like being in the half-buried lodges of some of the Growers. The few times I have been in one of those, it felt like a trap. I want to see where I am.

I had my armful of wood, and was making my way back to our camp, when I heard a noise beyond a clump of brush ahead. I stopped to see what it was, and moved ahead slowly, peering through the bushes. I didn't know what sort of animals might be found here.

There, I saw Toad, standing beside the mule. "Rabbit Horse," that mule was sometimes called, because of the long ears, you see. Now, I could not tell exactly what the boy was doing. He appeared to be stroking and grooming the mule's back, but when he touched a certain place on the flank, Rabbit Horse struck out suddenly with both hind feet. It was a curious thing, as if the mule had been taught to kick when he was touched at that place. Surely not, I told myself.

But then, after pondering for a moment, another thought occurred to me. Toad's idea of a joke on someone might be strange. Maybe, even, dangerous. Suppose he had taught the mule... Maybe he had noticed a kick such as this in reaction to a fly's bite, and touched or prodded at the same spot, to see whether the kick would be repeated.

Now, even as I watched, the youngster tickled the flank again with a stick. Again, Rabbit Horse's hind legs kicked out violently, straight to the rear. This could be a very touchy situation. I started to step into the open to reprimand Toad, but paused. A boy at this age, and one as unpredictable as Toad, was just ripe for trouble. His judgment was poor, and his ideas of what was funny, his sense of humor, was distorted, somehow. It was very immature. It is people such as this, I told myself, that give the Eastern band a bad reputation.

Yes, I see some of you smiling. I admit, my own judgment was not fully grown. Maybe it is not. But, this boy, I felt was in some way different in his thoughts. I always felt uncomfortable with Toad, as if I needed to watch him all the time. It is easy, I suppose, for you to think that my feelings were based on the fact that Toad interfered with my romantic desires. You would be right, of course.

Still, I felt a warning. It was strong enough that I did not make myself known. Toad was still grooming the mule as I backed quietly away, still wondering at this very different boy. I made my way back toward our camp. I tossed the firewood down, near where Dove was cooking.

It was not long before Toad appeared, and tied the mule near the other animals. He then led another of the horses, presumably to water. That was one of his chores, you see. In heavy woods such as the place we were camped, we did not turn the animals loose to graze. In open country, such as this where we are now, we could hobble a horse and turn it loose. In that country, the uneven land and thick timber make it necessary to tie them. You could not see them, thirty paces away.

I see that some of you are impatient for me to get on with my story. Let me tell it, please. It will take some time, because... Well, you will see. It cannot be hurried, because every detail is important. I, too, did not know it, then. I had no idea how important... I said nothing, but I resolved to watch Toad closely. Even his mischief could become dangerous. As I look back, it is well that I did so.

CHAPTER SIX

The next day we moved on, into an area not quite so rocky and uneven, and with more frequent areas of open grassland. Not like the Tallgrass Hills, of course, but more like lowlands surrounded by gentle hills and ridges. Not unpleasant country.

The people who live there, mostly Miss-our-ees and Osages, I think, live in towns, and grow corn and beans and pumpkins. Their meat is mostly deer. As we know, the buffalo stay in more open land. They do hunt turkeys, though. There are many more turkeys in such wooded country, but fewer of our prairie grouse.

Trading was good. At least, Lone Fox seemed the think so. This, you remember, was late summer. Fox was beginning to try to choose an area in which to winter. He told of big trading posts close to the Big River, the Miss-iss-ippi. It might be good, he thought, to camp near one of those, to watch what new goods would be available and which would be most desirable in trade. For the past season, he had traded fire strikers and knives, tobacco, sugar, beads, cloth, powder and lead, white man's things, for furs, quillwork and beaded shirts and moccasins and bags. Some furs, though he disliked untanned furs. Too bulky to pack. But well-tanned buckskins, and otter and fox were welcomed by the whites.

We were busy, and days followed quickly. In no time, it seemed, we were well into the Moon of Falling Leaves, white man's October.

Toad continued to be a great annoyance. Rarely, our various tasks, mine and the lovely White Plume's, were done, so that it might be possible to be alone. Such hopes were usually destroyed quickly. Toad took joy in following us, sometimes openly, making faces and taunting, teasing remarks. I was made to think his sister felt the same as I about her brother. *Aiee*, I would see his ugly face in my worst dreams.

Yes, you laugh, but I know that many have been in these situations. It is not good.

Sometimes, though, it became even worse. Toad would occasionally disappear. No, not that way... He did not simply vanish, though I sometimes suspected that he had enough evil medicine to have done it. No, in this matter, he sometimes was simply not anywhere. Of course White Plume and I suspected that he was hiding to spy on us from some place of concealment.

We would stroll off together, a little way into the woods, and it would seem natural for me to take White Plume's hand as we walked. Yet, to even touch her, if Toad was present, would bring hoots and calls of accusation. Not that I would have been misbehaving... Such an innocent gesture... Well, I see that you understand, some of you.

I became so occupied with these thoughts that sometimes I felt that maybe White Plume's parents had assigned Toad to spy on us. Then, when either parent would do me a kindness, I would feel ashamed to have suspected such a thing.

Thinking back, both thoughts were probably right. It may have been reassuring to White Plume's parents to feel that at least someone was in a position to keep us from becoming too foolish. All of this is simply to say that her parents approved of our friendship, at least in a limited way.

What? Yes, yes, I will go on. But it is needed that you understand what a disgusting little monster Toad could be.

The Moon of Falling Leaves seemed especially beautiful to me in that area. In the prairie, we see the change in the color of the grasses. The turkeyfoot grass, about the time of Cold Maker's first frost, becomes a dark reddish, the plume grass, yellow, and the little bluestem, a soft pink. The sumac is brightest red, but its leaves are quickly gone, to leave the others... Yes, I will go on, but this is a part of my story. In the country in which we found ourselves, the colors of ripening leaves on the trees are widely different, not only from those in the Tallgrass Hills, but from each other. Our cottonwoods turn bright yellow, and in the territory usually chosen for wintering by our Eastern band, some of the oaks and maples are brighter with reds of different shades.

In this new country, though, there were many different colors. Every tree and bush seemed to show a new color, from the palest yellow to deep blood red. You know the color of the liver of a fresh-killed buffalo, the red-brown? There was even that shade, in some of the thick forest growth. Mixed into all of this were patches of cedar, dark green on distant hillsides. Other shades of green, I saw in growths of pine forest.

Lone Fox explained to me that pines are not found in the prairie, though the western bands of the People see them in the mountains. He said that maybe the pines in the mountain are different than the ones we saw in the places where we were.

I tell you all of this to try to explain. There were things to come, so different from anything I had ever seen. I could not, and still cannot, decide... Were some of the things that happened because of the strange area where we were, or could they happen anywhere? That, I still find a dreadful thought. I dream, sometimes, of the Sacred Hills, the tallgrass country of the People, moving and rolling, rising and falling before my eyes, like a living thing, and the water rushing in...

Forgive me, my friends... This is not easy for me. When I think of some of the things my eyes have seen, it all comes rushing back, as the waters did. Give me a moment...

What? No, I can go on, my chief. Let me catch my breath... There, it is better now. I was saying... Yes, the colors, in the Moon of Falling Leaves. Different.

Maybe that difference was weighing heavily on me already, even before the Moon of Madness. I was occupied with the differences in the common things I saw. I could not tell, and I still cannot, just how much of the difference was due to where I was, and how much was due to the horrible things I was to see.

Either way, the warm, still days of the Second Summer passed, with the sights and smells of ripening. Days were becoming shorter, and squirrels were hurrying to store nuts. The bears and other creatures who avoid Cold Maker by sleeping were fattening on acorns, nuts, and berries. We avoided the bears, of course, as the People always have, because of our covenant with Bear. We do not hunt them, they do not hunt us.

Many of the birds were starting south. On the clear warm days, long lines of geese and ducks could be seen, honking their way south. The voices of the big gray geese were quite different from the smaller white snow geese, who fly higher, I noticed. Their call reminded me of a pack of small dogs barking in the distance. I think that I was impressed by this because there seemed to be more geese and ducks here than farther west. Fox, who has traveled widely, explained that the migrating flocks have roads in the sky which they travel, much as humans follow the trails on land.

"How are they marked, then?" I asked.

"No one knows," answered Fox, "but the birds do. It is a thing of the spirit, maybe."

It must be, I had to agree.

Now, I mention these things which are well known to all, because it was plain to see that the Moon of Madness was coming. The signs were clear: The migration of the waterfowl, the storing of winter supplies. Migrating buffalo were being hunted on the prairie, farther west, as always. As the days grow short, it comes to happen that all the creatures are beginning to act strangely. Birds who do not migrate seem to become confused. Of course, the year's hatch of quail and turkeys and grouse have never seen the trees when they are bare of leaves. They fly into what must seem to them to be open spaces, and sometimes are killed when they strike the bare branches.

The deer are entering the rutting season. Young bucks are polishing the fuzzy skin from their new antlers by attacking small trees. Even people in the plains have seen the shredded bark marking this practice combat. Maybe it was partly that I was in unfamiliar territory that made it only seem that there was something wrong. A dark shadow seemed to hang over the world. I know, you are aware of all this. But, try to see how I felt at the time. Something was not right. I felt it, yes. You wonder how I could have ignored it, but think of it. I was in strange country, different in itself. I knew that the Moon of Madness was at hand, but had no way to know whether it might be different in that region. Those facts could account for the complete surprise with which the coming events would fall on me.

CHAPTER SEVEN

Let me tell of some of the things I saw, which might have warned of events to come. Should have, I suppose, except that there seemed to be no real connection. I was ready to greet the Moon of Madness, as we do every year. I had, at that time, no hint that the Moon of Madness was to reach on and on, through the next four or five moons.

This seemed only a curious exception, then: At one of our night camps, we heard, out in the darkness of the forest, the rattle and clash of antlers, the snorts of the buck deer, engaged in combat. It was good. We were not in severe need but fresh meat would be welcome. We talked of this, and I was given permission for a short hunt the next morning. If it was successful we could delay for a day, to butcher out at least part of the meat. If not, we would move on. Simple, no?

I convinced Fox that Toad was to be closely observed and prevented from spoiling my hunt. I took my bow and two arrows. Probably I needed only one. There would be only one chance. Success, or a clean miss.

I worked my way, as silently as possible, in the direction where we had heard the struggle in the darkness of the night. I was moving very slowly and carefully. There were two bucks in the area. At least two, to have provoked the battle. The loser had probably fled the scene, but the winner would hang around to boast. It is rare, of course, but not unheard of, for a successful large buck to attack anything, even Man.

At about that time another thought struck me. I did not recall that I had ever been aware of such a battle at night. The few fights I had seen between buck deer had been in broad daylight. There was a lot of strutting and posing, threatening gestures and false charges, ending when the weaker or smaller of the two began to see the wisdom of retreat. All of these actions, however, would depend on the ability of the rivals to see each other...

I felt a cold chill on the back of my neck. This is not right, somehow, my thoughts warned.

At nearly the same moment, I heard a snort, the odd whistling noise that a suddenly alarmed deer makes sometimes. It came from very close, only a few steps away, and from the corner of my eye I saw a glimpse of motion. I froze, in an awkward stance, unwilling to move further before I had a chance to see what I was about to face. I even had some difficulty keeping my balance, one foot extended in a long stride, the other stretched out behind me. Later, I could laugh, but at that moment, things seemed pretty serious. Cautiously, I turned my eyes to the left, trying not to move another muscle.

It took a few moments for me to understand what I was seeing. The fact that I was peering through a patch of thick brush was no help, either. Another flash of movement, and I could make out the outline of a huge buck, head down and thrusting at some object on the ground in front of him. He was facing away from me, and it was hard to see beyond him.

Moving very slowly, I fitted an arrow to my bowstring, hoping for a clean heart or lung shot.

At about that time, the animal pivoted around, and for the first time I could see the situation clearly. There was not one buck, but two. One lay dead, and I could now see that the one still standing was the larger of the two. Understand, the other was not small. There were at least ten points on his antlers. Those of the larger buck numbered even more, and I now began to see the situation. In the course of the battle, the two had entangled their well branched weapons and had become bound together.

Aiee! I had heard of such things, but never had I seen it. They had struggled, neither able to quit the fight, until the weaker of the two could finally struggle no more. He was dead, but the victor was in a situation no better. He was doomed also.

The buck was exhausted, staggering, trying to pull free. This explained the sounds in the night.

You must bear with me on this next part, blaming my poor judgment on my youth and inexperience. I would never have admitted it at the time, due to that same youth and inexperience... Yes, you laugh, but there were times when there was nothing laughable, a you will quickly see. Let me go on.

Now, my eyes were showing me the opportunity of a lifetime, and I was seeing it completely wrong. I could have, with one arrow, killed the surviving buck, and could have told my grandchildren for many winters, how I had killed two deer with one arrow! It was an opportunity to camp another few days to smoke the venison, at least the best parts. The one had been dead only a short while, it appeared. It was still stiff and with spoilage would not be so. Besides, Fox. . . not the two-legged Lone Fox, but the four-legged fellow hunter who shares our kills since creation. . . Fox had not yet begun to harvest his share.

My attention, however, was turned to sympathy for the trapped buck. Through no fault of his own, in fact, because of his strength and skill as a warrior, he was facing death. He had counted coup on a worthy opponent. I hope you can follow my thoughts, here, and not think that I was completely stupid about it, though in truth, I was.

I walked nearer, bow still ready, looking at the tangled racks of antlers. It is impossible, in such a situation, to visualize exactly how it had happened. Somewhere in the tangle, there must be a single spur or fork which binds the two heads together. Cut or break that away, and the two heads are parted. Such logic flitted through my head like a butterfly in a field of blossoms. Think of it. I set my bow aside, took my ax from the belt at my waist and prepared to use it.

I could have, of course, used the weapon to kill the buck. One blow of the tomahawk. Did this even occur to me? Of course not. I was occupied with parting the two animals. I chose the more exposed antler on the head of the dead buck. If I could hack it loose from the skull, freeing the locked horns, my dilemma was ended, was it not? Ah, I see by your laughter that you see what I did not.

On the third or fourth blow to the dead buck's skull, there was a quick lunge on the part of the other. I was never sure exactly how it happened. The buck, exhausted and near death from his efforts and from starvation, suddenly found new life. I caught only a glimpse of an antler with a bloody base, tossed into the air, before I was flattened by the animal's rush. I do not know how I escaped being impaled on the sharp points. Somehow, I managed to drop the ax and grab the slashing antlers. The buck swung his head from side to side, swinging me against the brush and trees. Though not exactly impaled, I was still being gored across my chest and shoulders. I had to hold on, because the slashing tines were already far too close to my face, especially my eyes. I closed them tightly, although I knew that it would be of no help if one of those points struck an eye socket. As you see, it did not, though my smile is a little lopsided, maybe, by a chance blow from a sharp point which I did not even feel at the time.

I was growing weaker, the world seem to go dark. I heard a woman screaming, someone running through the fallen leaves, and then I felt a crushing weight on my chest. My last thought before complete blackness came over me was: So this is how it feels to die.

CHAPTER EIGHT

I did not know how badly I was injured at first. I woke with the feeling that every part of my body was painful. That was just when I lay still. When I tried to move, *Aiee!* Even to blink my eyelids was painful. My left eye was swollen shut, and there was a heavy ache across my left shoulder. When I tried to move it, the ache changed to burning, stabbing pain. I must have moaned, because White Plume appeared suddenly at my side, touching my face gently. I could see her look of concern, and that, at least, was good. About the only good thing, maybe, except that I was alive, and there was a little while that I questioned that theory. But, I reasoned, the dead do not feel pain, so I must be alive. There were few parts of my body that did not throb with the slightest movement. I drifted off.

When I woke again it was night, which was confusing to me. Surely, the day was still young. But as I gradually began to relate to the world of the living, I realized that the whole day had passed.

It must be early evening, because the fire had not yet burned low. I tried to turn my head to look around, setting off spasms of pain in the muscles of my neck and shoulders. I moaned, and White Plume was there beside me again.

"Lie still," she crooned softly, stroking my cheek with a light touch.

That was wonderful, but I was ashamed to have her see me in such condition. I was young, you know. Yes, I still am. But at that time I still carried the idea that I should be trying to impress the girl with my strength and wisdom and all the other skills she might seek in a man. You see, I had not yet learned that what a woman wants in a man, what she sees and what she needs are all different. They have very little relation to each other. Somehow it is made to be that these facts are carefully kept from a young man at the time he needs to know them. It is the way of things, maybe. But, at that time, you cannot know what strong medicine there was in the gentle touch of her hands.

There was a slight distraction when Toad appeared, and my heart jumped. In my helpless condition, it could not be a good thing to have this troublemaker near me. I must have moaned at the thought, and White Plume soothed me with soft words and soft touch. She would protect me, I realized, from any actual danger from her brother. This did not help much, as I thought of how exposed I would be to Toad's clever mischief. White Plume could not be with me all of the time, and when she was absent... You can understand my dread, no? There were many things Toad might contrive to make my life miserable.

For some reason I thought of a thing I had once seen. I had been watching a brood of kittens, which I had discovered in a hollow tree near where my parents were camped. There were three of them; fat, soft and amusing as they played. I was well hidden, and enjoyed their comical pretended fierceness.

Then their mother returned, a large spotted cat, the short-tailed kind. She carried a good-sized pack rat, and I saw that it was still alive. She dropped it near her brood, and the rat tried to run. The kittens stared stupidly. The mother cat caught it again in one jump, brought it back, and released it again. She was teaching them, you see...

What? No, it has nothing to do with my story, except that I felt as the pack rat must have as the plaything of those kittens. I was helpless, and I did not know for how long. Toad might find many ways to make my life miserable. I could not move, and had no idea when I could even sit or stand. I am only trying to explain my feelings of helplessness.

As for actual injuries, yes, I was battered and stiff. Every muscle made its own protest when I attempted so much as a deep breath.

The gash over my left eye had now pulled apart again from the swelling. I could tell by gently touching that the wound was stretched open. Someone had removed my shirt, bloodied in several places where the buck had counted coup on me before Fox killed it with an arrow.

Dove had rummaged among their personal luggage and produced a gourd container, filled with a salve of some sort. She applied it gently to the cut over my eye, and to the injuries on my chest and shoulder. There were several deep puncture wounds, and my ribs throbbed from the force of the thrust of horn striking bone, where they had collided. Probably one or two ribs were cracked, on the left. But that was good. Far better than if the tine of an antler had slipped between the ribs to puncture a lung. I would not be here today!

At this point I want to say again how grateful I was. I still am. If the parents of White Plume, the trader and his wife, had not taken charge of my battered carcass, I probably would not be here at all. Fox, except for me and my injuries, would have been on down the trail. They could have abandoned me, and as helpless as I was, I might have been dead by now. Much sooner, probably. It had not yet occurred to me that they were losing a large part of the season's trade because of me. I did repeatedly express my thanks, which effort was brushed aside.

No man is comfortable to be seen as weak and helpless by a woman whose bed he hopes to share. That bothered me considerably, but White Plume seemed to take joy in my weakness. Her motherly instincts, I suppose. A woman is hard to understand at best, and with my inexperience and my injuries, I was trying to fight several battles at once. Not the least of these was the remorse for the trouble I had caused for everyone, including my own parents.

Fox and Dove did take advantage of the opportunity to dress out the carcass of the buck which had nearly killed me. That meat was fresh and good, though they decided against trying to salvage any of the flesh of the other animal. The weather was warm, and the flies were drawn to the scent. Fox dragged that carcass downwind for the distance of a bow shot or two, with the aid of one of the horses.

The better carcass, fresh-killed, was of good quality. A bit tougher than that of a fat yearling, maybe, but quite usable for drying. Dove was skilled in preparation of the thin strips, spread on a rack of willow sticks near the fire... On the downwind side, in this case. The smoke would not only keep flies away, but add some flavor to the drying meat. The dried and smoked strips would be simply stored for later use, to be cooked in soups or stews. They could, of course, be chewed without further preparation, or pounded with tallow and dried berries to make pemmican, at any time later.

I was learning, you see. I had seen my mother preparing foodstuffs many times, but... Well, that had been commonplace. I had not really observed in a manner to understand what I was watching. How different, to watch the same tasks performed by White Plume and her mother. Maybe I was beginning to learn, at least a little. It was to be hoped, because at that time I had a long way to go. Yes, I still do, but then, I had not yet even located the trail.

We were camped there ten sleeps or more, maybe half a moon, before moving on. It was a day or two before I could sit up for more than a short while. Standing, or attempting to, was one of the most difficult tasks at hand. I stood, swaying like a willow in the wind, wondering if I would ever be able to walk normally again. I was determined not to let my weakness show, but that was a futile effort. I had to admit it, because if for no other reason, it was so painfully obvious. Once again, I was embarrassed before the most important person in my life, and in the presence of her parents.

Somehow, I survived the pain, faintness, and embarrassment, and in a few more days I began to gain strength. At last, I thought, maybe I can survive this, after all.

Moon of Madness

CHAPTER NINE

Through all of this injury and weakness as I healed from the battering I had experienced, I worried about Toad. I still felt that he was longing to play tricks on me while I was nearly helpless. Possibly he was being prevented from acting on such impulse only by the presence of his parents. And White Plume, of course.

I was still very weak, and would have been unable to defend myself if Toad decided to act on some of the dangerous pranks that I was certain he had in mind.

So, I remained uneasy. Especially so, on an occasion or two. Once I wakened to find him bending over me. No one else was in sight. Toad was holding a stalk of one of the grasses which grow there, one with a fuzzy seed head. He had been tickling my nose, knowing that I would probably jump as I woke, and that it would be annoying and painful for me to do so. This, you see, was how Toad's twisted sense of humor often surfaced.

I did jump, and it did hurt, and he laughed, long and loud. His parents or White Plume would have prevented such a thing, but Toad did such things only when they were not present. I should have told them what was happening, I suppose, but it would have seemed childish on my part, would it not?

What if I had said "Toad has been abusing me. He has tickled my nose with a fuzzy grass stem?"

Ah, you see! I did have a problem, no? I had no desire to make myself look foolish, or weak, or intolerant of childish pranks. It was only that I did not know how far Toad might carry it. I might have felt better, even, if he had done his little tricks when the others were present. The fact that he wanted them to see what he was doing made me very uneasy. Yes, some of you laugh, but you may never have been in such a situation.

I was improving daily, and it would not be long until our party could move on. I regretted the fact that Fox had lost so much trading time because of my accident. I tried to apologize, but both he and Dove brushed it aside.

"Anyone would do the same," Fox insisted.

I knew better, and they knew that I knew, which was important.

"If not for you, we would not have this large supply of dried meat!" the trader assured me, a glint of humor in his eyes. That part, at least, was true.

There was one other thing which happened while we were still camped there, which I did not understand at the time. Looking back, I am made to think that it did have meaning.

We were moving into a time and place that would involve strange happenings. There were to come many things that we did not understand. Some, surely, not meant to be understood. We were to meet many people, of other tribes and nations, some of which have very strange and different ways. Maybe I am making no sense at all, but I must try.

With all of these different customs which we were to encounter, it was, and still is, very hard to say what might have carried meaning. And after all, who is to say? When some event happens, and is seen by those with different customs... Ah! Let me tell it this way: The People do not kill or eat bears, no? This is because of our covenant with Bear, since Creation. We do not hunt Bear, and Bear does not hunt us. But some, like our friends and allies, the Head Splitters, have no such agreement with Bear. To them, bear meat is delicious. Is it not so? Whether our friends eat bear meat is their problem, between them and the bear, and not ours to question.

I may not be telling this clearly, but I must try, because so many of the events to come were so strange. And, some of the people we met were strange, also, with strange ways.

But, there was a thing that happened while we were still camped at the place the bucks fought. An owl came. To us, the People, Owl is a messenger, and may carry good news, or warnings. We respect and honor him. To others, Owl may be the carrier of bad luck. Some, as we know, may try to kill any owl, because of the bad tidings he may carry.

On the last night where we had camped while I began to heal, there came an owl. Not one of the little owls, whose voice is much like the chuckling call of the raccoon. This was the big one, with ears like those of a cat. Kookooskoos, the hunter.

I heard him in the woods just at sundown, calling his own name with a hollow cry. Good hunting, Uncle, I sent the thought-message back toward him.

We heard his call again, several times that evening, as he moved through the darkening woods, searching for a kill. Rabbit, probably. I have always liked to hear his hunting call. It makes me feel, somehow, that all is well.

It was fully dark, and a rising moon shone through the grove of slim trees to the east of our fire. Suddenly a silent shadow floated across our camp, its wings not moving. As the owl neared a giant oak, it rose in a long graceful curve to land on one of the lower branches. Then the bird turned, and I felt that I was honored by the fact that it seemed to look directly at me.

"Ah, this is bad!" muttered Dove.

It took me a moment to realize that among her people, as well as others, the attention of the owl may not be something to be sought. To some, Owl is the messenger of death, of bad things to come. How can this be? I wondered. Of course there could be no answer. Some things are not intended to be understood, and this was one of the things of the spirit-world.

These ideas were still scurrying through my head in a scramble of confused thoughts when I heard, almost beside me, the twang of a bowstring. I was still looking at the owl, who now appeared to be knocked backward from his perch on the oak tree, as if an invisible hand had swatted him like a fly.

"No!" I yelled as I turned to look.

Almost at my left elbow stood Toad, his bow still in position, after having released the arrow.

"What... why..?" I muttered helplessly.

Looking back, I am sometimes made to think that this was the beginning of all the strange happenings that were to follow us for the next several moons. Then I remember that no, it began with the fighting buck deer and their locked horns, even before that. The Moon of Madness... *Aiee*, my brothers and sisters! Give me a moment, to steady myself...

Yes, it was the Moon of Madness. But never could we have imagined that the Moon of Madness would last for the next four moons, as it was to be.

I was more concerned at the time with Toad's action in killing the owl. I had not quite realized yet that in the ways of his people, Toad had done a brave and noble thing.

How could this be? If I had killed an owl, the messenger, among our People, it would have been a very bad action on my part. But in the ways of Toad's tribe, that of his mother, it seemed right and proper, a good thing to have done.

I was beginning to learn, you see, that I had no right to make decisions for Toad, what he should do. Each tribe or nation must follow its own ways, no? But at that time, I was still confused.

Fox tried to help me learn, that evening at the fire. He was skilled in such matters, as he dealt constantly with people of different beliefs.

"You are troubled about the owl?" Fox asked me.

We were alone near the fire, the others somewhere else, preparing for the night.

"Of course!"

I probably snapped at him, because I was upset.

Fox nodded agreement, and was quiet for a little while.

"Your people honor the Owl, no?" he said finally.

"That is true."

I wondered where this conversation was going.

"Then you, too, should do so."

"But Toad... "

"Ah, yes! Toad is not of your tribe. But should he too follow the ways of his people, as you follow yours?"

I was rapidly becoming confused now, but Fox continued.

"Toad has followed his mother's way. That is the custom among her people."

"You mean that he follows her ways, or that the owl is an enemy?"

"Both, maybe. My own people see Owl much like yours do, as a helpful messenger."

"But," I blurted indignantly, "Does it not worry you that Toad kills the messenger?"

"That is Toad's problem, not mine," said Fox calmly. "I cannot tell him what he thinks. It is his to choose which path he follows, and he chose that of his mother's people.

I was now beginning to understand, at least partly. Each tribe and nation has its own ways, which should be respected by all, though we may not agree.

I must think more about this, I realized. As I drifted off to sleep, still puzzling about Owl, another thought came to me. The messenger had been killed before he had the chance to make more than a first contact. The question that I now faced was far more complicated than I had thought.

What was the message that had been carried by the now dead messenger? I had no idea.

CHAPTER TEN

We moved on, heading eastward, following a well-traveled trail. I was beginning to gain back some strength, but it was very slow. I gradually came to be more aware of my surroundings, rather than merely my own aches and pains.

In the course of all this, I began to fully realize for the first time what a sacrifice Fox and his family had made for me. They had lost half a moon's trading just to look after me and my injuries, which were mostly my own fault anyway.

Consider now, that the trading season is limited to the seasons when the weather allows travel. My injuries had caused Fox to lose a substantial part of his summer's gain. I would need to be very helpful and considerate. I did voice my thanks, but it was brushed aside. It was apparent that actions rather than words would be the appropriate thanks to the trader's family for the saving of my life. If not for them, I would have died in the woods.

I am made to think now that I was beginning to think as a man, rather than a child. That is a change that we cannot see until long after it happens. It takes a close encounter with death, maybe, to even begin to learn. Even then, it is only when we look back that we realize: That was a narrow escape

It is an important step, and I felt that I had grown in wisdom. Yes, maybe only a little, but it was a start.

I had a harder time in trying to relate to Toad. Until then, he had been an immature, childish tease. Dangerous, maybe, because of his immaturity and his lack of ability to see what might become serious if not handled sensibly. I had not yet begun to forgive him for his intrusion into my romantic connection with White Plume.

Even that, however, was overshadowed by Toad's killing of the owl. I could listen to Fox's explanation; I could understand that among Dove's people, such a kill was something to take pride in. Still, to me it did not seem right. It would have been too much to expect me to grow up all at once, no?

I avoided contact with Toad when I could, possibly the wrong approach. Maybe it would have been better to talk seriously with him. I would never have believed anything so ridiculous at that time, though. But as I look back, yes. Toad, too, was in the process of maturing, as I was myself. But I saw the youngster mostly as an obstacle to my romantic ambitions. Can there be anything as annoying to a young couple whose romance is warming? Under other circum-stances, I might have tolerated Toad. Possibly, even, enjoyed his company as a hunting companion, though his tricks and practical jokes... I could not forget his teaching the mule to kick. I still did not understand the deliberate teasing and annoying of the animal. It was too much of a stretch for the imagination that I could ever relate well to this person.

Now so far, I have not mentioned any of the people we had met as we moved into unfamiliar country. It seems that there was actually a considerable amount of travel going on. Among the People, when we say "travel" it means the movement of one of the bands, under the leadership of that band's chieftain. A move to a new hunting area, maybe, or to an area of better grass to feed the horse herds.

I was learning quickly about other reasons for travel. That of the trader, for instance, or someone on a vision quest, or maybe, among some, just for curiosity. Or, as in my own case, romance. *Aiee*, how childish I was!

In the area where we were now traveling, there were more permanent lodges than movable ones. Some were much like those of the Growers in our Tallgrass Hills. Some were dug halfway into the ground, others built of logs or stone or clay. Sometimes there would be a town of several of these lodges.

We met several tribes, some of which we already knew. Kaw or Kansa. They are the same, Fox told me. Osage, Miss-our-ee, Sac and Fox. Most of these are Growers, at least part of the time, and maybe they have a fall hunt for buffalo out onto the prairie.

There were also whites, of several different tribes. I had always supposed that a white man is a white man. They all look alike, no? It seems, though, that there are several kinds, with different tongues. Fox told me of this. They come from different parts of the white man's world. Some talk a tongue called Yen-glees, another may use Francois, and of course, our own Mountain bands have traded with the whites in Sennafay. Whites talk each others' tongues sometimes, and those who trap for furs also use hand signs and speak some of our languages.

Yes, you know all this, but I tell it as a background for what else we found. There are many of the native people who are moving west to get away from the whites. There are more and more whites, it is said, everywhere to the east. They fight with each other, and with anybody, apparently.

They have this odd custom, a belief that somehow it is possible to buy or sell a place. Then if it is possible to own it, as a possession like a horse or a lodge or a weapon, then is it not also possible to steal it?

This, we were told, is what goes on far to the east, where the whites grow more and more in numbers. Already, they try to push out some who live there. Oh, yes... Most of the whites are those whose tongue is Yen-gleese. They have fought with the Francois and driven them to the north. The others, those in the south, speak the tongue of those we have traded with in Sennafay.

Yes, I know... I am trying to explain, but there are many things, and in a strange mixture. It is important, a part of what happened. Let me tell it!

You know that there are people from several of the tribes and nations who live to the east, who have come into our region just to get away from the whites. Some of them have joined us on the plains, and are good friends to the People. Is there not a medicine woman in the Southern band, called "Snakewater?" Her people are from the east, called Tsallagee, or "Cherokee."

Yes, they are among those being crowded out by the white-eyes. But there are others, too. We talked to several different travelers. You see, among the whites, those who speak the Yen-gleese tongue, are the most powerful. They have fought among themselves, but now want to fight everybody else, and push all others, even the other whites, out of the land that they want. They want all the native tribes and nations to move to the west, and they offer gifts to those who would go. Money, a place to live...

Ah, someone asks where this is to be? There is an area to the south and east of the country we know. It is called Ar-kansa, that is, "downstream" from the Kansa people, the Growers of our prairie.

We met people of several tribes and nations, all heading west. Some were going to this Ar-kansa, where some of them are already living. It seemed to us that each nation is split over this. Well, the Cherokees... Some of them think the move a good idea, away from the whites without shedding blood. Others say no, fight! Kill the whites! Still others say no, adopt the ways of the whites, join them. Every tribe or nation has those who argue both ways. They fight among themselves.

There are those who argue that this happens because it is part of the white man's medicine. They can cast a spell that causes men to fight their own people. I don't know, but that has been said.

What? Are there no leaders, you ask? Maybe too many. That may be part of the spell, to create too many who want to lead. But let me go on.

Many Cherokees had already moved to this Ar-kansa, we were told by other Cherokees heading that way. We also saw a town, much like that of whites, Fox said, built by Chickamaugas from the east, from back near the Cherokees.

There were others, too. Creeks, the long time enemies of the Cherokees. We were told of a powerful holy man of the Shawnees, yet another of the eastern nations. His name is Tecumseh. He has taught that the only way to stop the trouble is to return to the old ways, to give up everything that has been introduced by the whites.

He would send word, he had told the Creeks, as to when they must do this, and at the same time everybody must rise up and begin to kill whites. Of course, there are many who would not agree. Some of the white man's things are too handy. Guns, fire strikers, metal knives. The wide assortment of beads, and needles with which to sew, canvas for lodge covers.

Tecumseh had become angry over this, we were told, and placed a curse on those present, and on the whole area, where we were, as he departed to go back to his own people. As he left, he had a threat. When he reached his own people, he said, he would stamp his foot, and the whole earth would shake. That would signal the time to rise up and kill whites, and those who would not help would regret it.

I was to think of that later.

We were told of another prophet, a Cherokee, maybe, who traveled with two black wolves. Some thought them to be spirit-beings. This man, Tsali, taught that a storm with big hailstones would come, to kill all who did not follow him. He would lead his followers to a mountain top to wait for the world's end.

I was to remember that, too.

Now, I have been telling of all these things, because they seemed to fall into place, and to make sense, much later. And yes, I know that anyone who sees anything sensible about this may be bordering on madness himself... Give me a moment, here... This is not easy for me. There have been times, I thought that I must be going mad.

Where was I? Oh, yes... I'll go on.

We were seeing clusters of lodges, as I said. Some were whites, others were some of the native people who had taken whites' ways. Many were mixed families, maybe a white trapper and his Indian wife. Some of the settlements of Cherokee or Creek might have a white trapper or two who had taken the ways of the wife's people.

Now there has been much talk about "white man's ways," and returning to the "old ways." I am made to think that it would be hard to decide which old ways. As I have said, some things of the white man have been good. Some will argue, but each of us must have a point at which we say yes, this is good, but everything else, bad. Where do we draw that line?

I was thinking of this as I saw many of the white man's customs followed by the assorted mixture of people who lived there. One thing, which much surprised me, was the assortment of animals that they keep. Among the People, we have had dogs since creation, it is said. Our ancestors used them to carry or to drag packs when they moved. Then ate them sometimes when the hunt was poor, as we do now. That was before we had horses, of course. Horses now do the carrying and dragging and are ridden on the hunt, as well. To war, if needed.

We know mules, too, the "rabbit-eared horse." The whites not only ride horses and mules, and use them to pack and to pull the pole-drag, but to pull what is called a "wagon" in their tongue. It is like a big wooden box, but on each corner is a round wheel, much like the rolling part on some of our toys. It turns on an axle. It is much easier to pull a wagon than a pole-drag, of course, but it needs a good road. Many of the trails are too narrow or too rough.

But I had started to tell of their animals. Whites have dogs, like ours, but also other creatures. There is one kind, much like a buffalo, but spotted and striped or of almost any color. They kill these for meat sometimes, but also they squeeze milk from the bag of the nursing female. Yes, it is true, and the animals are easily handled, as calm and gentle as an old mare. There are yet other animals, too. One is covered with tightly curled fur, which can be cut off and used to make cloth. The animal is called "sheep," and it can be eaten, too.

Another is called "pig," and some that I saw were very fat and greasy. The taste is good, though. They will eat almost anything, it is said.

Besides all these are a small cat, about the size of a rabbit, with a long tail. They could be eaten, I suppose, but I never saw it. These cats live in the lodges of the whites sometimes, and are said to catch mice.

Oh, yes, I nearly forgot. There are several kinds of birds used by the whites. Ducks, geese, and an odd creature like a grouse, of different shapes and sizes, which they keep mostly for the eggs they lay. They are called "chickens."

What? Do these birds fly away? They do not seem to do so, and this was puzzling to me, too. Maybe there is a spell or conjure of some sort. They are kept in cages sometimes.

But what I wanted to tell was that many of the natives who live near the white settlements are keeping pigs, cows, and sheep or some of the birds. If they followed the advice of some of those who call themselves prophets, they would have to give up not only the tools and weapons of the whites, but pigs, sheep, cattle, and chickens. And, what about horses? They were first brought by whites, no? If they give up all of the white man's ways, there could be some hard decisions. Give up the horse? Pigs?

Cows? I am made to think that there would be no place to stop. Each of us would have different thoughts. I could give up pigs, but not my horse. Or: A gun is too noisy anyway, but I must have my metal knife, or axe or whatever.

I began to see many of the problems in mixing with the white man's ways. I was seeing it as it was happening. It was much different. I had not known what to expect, but nothing like what I was seeing there. Still very few people, and those getting along without many problems. When there are very few, they help each other, because they have to. I was learning, you see. I had a long way to go, but it was a start. I began to notice things that had not become a problem, but could be expected to do so. Well, like pigs and chickens. With more people in less space, they might eat someone else's crops.

I am only trying to explain the place and the people we found there, and what they thought might become problems. I have come to think, though, that we all worry about the wrong things. That which causes us grief or danger or sadness is always the unexpected, not that over which we worried, no?

But yes, I will go on. We were camped near a white men's town that was called, in their tongue, "New Madrid." Their names are strange, no? "New," we can translate, but I have no idea what a "madrid" might be. Maybe a tool or a weapon. It might even be another of their animals, which I did not happen to see, before the trouble started. And after that, *Aiee!* There was no chance to even wonder about such simple things as a town's name.

Fox was doing a little trading, though not much. It was mostly a white town, and they could buy things from other whites to the north or east.

He planned to move south into Ar-kansa, to test the possibility of trading with those arriving from the east, Cherokees and Creeks and others. But it was not to be.

I have spoken of the prophets and the arguments and predictions, and how the people of some of the tribes were fighting among themselves. Some were predicting terrible things, but no one had seen how bad it could really be.

CHAPTER ELEVEN

The day the madness began was clear and sunny. One of the late autumn days, cool and sharp but not uncomfortable. There was little wind. In my own mind, I have always connected that day with the Moon of Madness, because of the madness that followed. In truth, it was a little past the Mad Moon, and a few days into the Moon of Long Nights, the white man's December, when it happened.

I had been looking for firewood for Dove's cooking fire. I was still stiff and sore with the beating I had taken from the big buck. They had decided that it might be good to winter in this area. Possibly a little farther south; there were still travelers on the trail, and Fox was taking advantage of the opportunity to trade.

A problem in any settlement of this sort, a town, is firewood. All of the dead wood in a circle around the center has been used, and it is necessary to go farther for fuel. A town of people who stay there all the time, instead of moving as the People do, they have to plan ahead for firewood. Well, as we do in winter camp. So, I was gathering wood.

Yes, I will get back to the story! But this does relate to it. The firewood... You see, most of the lodges in this town were of logs or stones, piled up in a square and with a roof over it, of one kind or another. The whites use a different kind of smoke hole on their lodges, which I do not understand. There is no way to move any flaps to adjust the opening as we have on our lodges, so that it will draw the smoke when the wind changes. But downwind is usually east, so it seems not to matter too much.

I have to describe a little more, now. In the lodges of the whites, they build a place for fire, of stones and clay. The "fire place." It is closed on three sides, and the smoke is forced to flow straight up, through a squarish tunnel, like a hollow tree. I wondered if this entrapment might be displeasing to the spirits. Maybe, even, a cluster of such houses, with confinement of its spirits... Could this possibly have caused the disaster? I thought of that later.

But, to go on. These hollow smoke logs are made simply of stones and clay. The clay bakes hard from the rising heat. Some are even made of sticks and clay. I thought that was not such a good idea, but it seemed to work.

These "chimneys," as they call the smoke pipe, are made to stand up higher than the top of the house. This, I suppose, to carry sparks away on the wind. I have gone to this detail to give you a look at what I saw that morning.

I need to pause to say that, in truth, the Moon of Madness which had begun earlier seemed trapped in place somehow. When it should have been ending, it was just beginning, though there was no way to know it at that time. How could anyone know that the madness was just about to start, and would last so long? Who ever heard of the madness becoming active not for one moon, but more than four, stretching entirely through the winter? The moons of Long Nights, Snows, and Hunger; even into the new year, the Moon of Awakening, called "March" by the white man. Oh, forgive me... The memory still makes me shake sometimes.

I am made to think there were some who knew. That morning there was a sort of heavy feel to the day. Birds, squirrels and other creatures, usually active on such a morning, were quiet. A hawk, circling high above, screamed down at the quiet town. I could not have told then, and cannot, even now, why I felt as I did, but the other creatures seemed to feel something, too. Dogs were restless. I saw none simply sleeping in the sun, as we would expect on a still, sunny day after a frosty night.

Horses were restless, too, seeming not to be able to browse or eat their fodder without pausing to jump and look around at something unseen by humans. As you see, it is hard to explain even now, when we know what happened next.

There was no warning. A low, rumbling sound, like that of a buffalo stampede when the great herds migrate through our Tallgrass Hills. It seemed that the earth shivered a little under our feet.

It took a few moments to realize that in the area where we were, there were no buffalo to create such a stampede. There were buffalo, yes, but not in great numbers. Smaller bands, rarely more than a hundred, maybe.

The rumbling became a little heavier, and I looked around me to try to see where it came from. I was standing at the west end of the little town, looking east. The road wound between the lodges, and I could see nearly to the other side of the town. I was having trouble with my eyes... I could not seem to get a clear look at anything. You know how it feels, in deep cold or a strong wind? It was like that. The shapes of distant houses and trees seemed to wiggle and squirm. As I said, I was afraid that I was about to go blind. Everything in my vision was writhing and squirming... Ah, I know! You recall how a nest of maggots looks a day or two after the butchering is finished, at a big kill? The whole world was squirming like that. Not in really big heaves, but just barely wiggling. My head told me that this cannot be, that lodges built of logs and stone cannot move.

But, they were moving, swaying, squirming. I could see a hillside quivering, too, but an odd thing... there was smoke puffing from the stone and clay smoke pipes, the chimneys. One of those about a bowshot away from me, down the road, a chimney of stone, suddenly shattered and fell. The dust that followed seemed to tell me... the puffs of smoke that I had seen must have been puffs of dust instead, as the clay turned to powder.

The house where the chimney had fallen now seemed to fold in on itself. The roof fell in. The sides were still standing. This one was made of logs, and one corner began to sag, and fell in on itself.

Then, real smoke began to curl up through the tangle of logs. I could be sure about this, because it was white, the smoke from burning wood. The dust puffs had been a dirty brown from the clay that held the thing together.

The rumbling had stopped, and the earth had stopped shaking. The feeling of having no balance was gone. For the space of a few heartbeats, there was dead silence. Then, sounds began to be heard again. A dog barked. Someone called out, probably a name, though in a tongue I did not know. It was, I thought, probably a mother, trying to locate a child.

From another direction, a woman screamed, and that sound changed into a high-pitched yell. I could not tell whether it was a mourning song, or just a wail of terror. People were running, calling to each other.

I started toward our camp, passing between houses that appeared untouched and those that were flattened. Nearly all had suffered some damage, though. It crossed my mind that we were fortunate not to have a lodge that was fastened to the earth, but one that was movable. Our way, that of the People, with lodges that can be picked up and carried, was surely the best, in this situation.

It will seem odd, that I had a little trouble finding our camp. With some of the houses flattened, and a few large trees down... Oh, yes! I had not told of the trees. Some had fallen. Only the big ones. Small trees stood untouched, as they had bent easily and recovered. The weight of the big oaks and other kinds had caused them to fall. One had fallen straight across a house, and people were scrambling out through the door, a window, and over broken logs, yelling in terror.

I do not know how long it was... I had not yet reached the camp, when the shaking began again. I was made to think that it was harder and heavier, but maybe not. Maybe it was only that I experienced it, and dreaded its return.

I was still trying to keep my balance, and dreading what might happen next, when I happened to look up, past and over the little town. I thought my eyes were playing tricks on me again.

A hill, a few bowshots beyond the houses, appeared alive. The entire hillside began to slide, and thundered into the valley below. I could not believe my own eyes. A cloud of dust rose from the fallen rocks and dirt as it filled the little valley.

I remember thinking that the stream which flowed along the base of the hill would be blocked. It was a horrible feeling. Earth itself was breaking up. There was no place to hide, or to run, to escape the terror.

CHAPTER TWELVE

I have tried to tell you how the earth shook, though it cannot really be told. You would have to be there to know how it felt. I told of the dust puffing up as the log houses fell, and how it appeared like smoke when the clay crumbled. I did not see how things could be worse.

There was no way to tell that this was only the beginning.

People were still calling the names of those missing. Most of them turned up, some hurt, maybe bleeding. One woman was dead, crushed in the fall of her house.

Except for the things I have told, that was about all on the first day. People were afraid to go to where the top of the hill slid down. There were a few quiet shudders that evening, but no big shaking.

Toward afternoon there were some frightened travelers who came, looking for a safe place to stay. That was almost funny. Who could know? It seemed that it would be safer to stay out of the houses, but the weather was cold and would soon be colder, maybe. Those with canvas lodges were fortunate.

Dove and Fox were experienced in finding a way to shelter themselves and their family. It seemed that there was no advantage in trying to travel until the tremors stopped. Not many would be interested in trading. So, we worked to improve our camp, cutting a few poles to enlarge the lean-to we had made when we arrived there.

I asked about their winter plans. Fox had expected to bargain for a lodge cover, maybe a teepee, poles and all; or, a canvas tent, though it would not be very handy. The white man's tents have no smoke flaps, so there can be no fire. Dove would have to cook outside, and winter was coming. But for now, there was no reason to move.

The reaction of people to this event was widely different. Toad, for instance, actually seemed disappointed that he had not caused the event. I was irritated by his behavior, but realized that considering his strange behavior in normal times, this was probably to be expected. Maybe I even recognized that at his age I too might have laughed over the sliding down of the hilltop. It was such an impossible occurrence that it seemed untrue, an act of mischief like that of a joke. And to Toad, everything was a joke.

White Plume's behavior was pleasing to me. She showed an expected amount of concern, and seemed to want to stay close to me. That was good. It also helped, probably. I did not want to show fear or concern, but to appear to White Plume as a mature and capable man, a good prospect as possible husband material. I had to remain calm and stable, no?

As for Fox and Dove, they had been through enough life experience, good and bad, to stay calm, though concerned. Their life as a trader's family had prepared them for almost anything. This in turn had a calming effect on me, I suppose. It was good, for me to be with people of this kind at this time of my life.

After those first shocks there had been little travel on the road, except for the few who straggled in, confused and weary. Everyone had a story to relate, where they were and what they were doing when the first rumble came; what it looked like to them. These stories were told over and over. It was as if even those telling them did not really believe what they had seen and what had happened to them.

There was one couple, a man and wife, who staggered in just before dark. The husband's face was one big puffy mass, like a misformed pumpkin. His eyes were swollen shut, and his lips were like ripe plums, round and shiny.

They had no packs.

Their pack horse had panicked at the first rumbles, the wife told. The animal had run blindly into the woods, the man chasing after it. Man and horse, unfamiliar with the area, blundered into a cedar tree which held a hornets' nest. The big round melon-shaped nest. This one was huge. Both were stung many times, and the horse broke away and disappeared. The man's eyes were swelling so quickly that by the time he realized that he could not follow the horse, he could hardly see. They came back together, the man and wife, by calling out to each other. Now they had nothing, and the man was very sick from the stings.

Somebody, maybe a relative or someone from the same tribe, took them in. This was only one of the many stories that were told and retold.

There was one which I did not even believe at the time. That is an area of many springs, you know. Fresh, sweet water comes out of the ground, sometimes in great amounts, mixing with other springs to make streams and rivers of clear, cold water. That much we know to be true. But this one man told of a strange happening. When the shaking of the earth happened, he said, he saw a stream of water that instead of trickling and falling down, shot up, into the air. People tried to tell him no, water does not spurt up, it falls or tumbles down. He described what he saw as like a waterskin with a hole in it. Squeeze such a skin, and water squirts up, through the hole, does it not? It was like that, the man insisted, a stream shooting straight up, higher than the tallest trees! And remember, there are trees there which are ten times the height of a man.

What? Did I believe it? I had my doubts, I confess. But let me go on.

I had told you of the many different people, and of different tribes, who were traveling across that area at the time. Some were related loosely to each other, some were strangers, some were traditional enemies, even. It was already an area of great tension. Add the tension of these strange happenings... *Aiee!* At one point I wondered if it was possible that all of the pressure caused by these conflicts could be causing these disasters.

Tecumsah had, in anger, sworn to stamp his foot, and "the earth will shake." Most people had thought that the leader spoke in terms of the spirit, not of the stones and dirt. But who knows what a seer of his reputation might have intended.

There was one leader who had lost his reputation and his power, though it was true that this might not have been connected to the quakes. Tsali, the Cherokee, self-proclaimed prophet, had predicted a disaster, but at a different place, a different time, and of a different sort. He had gathered with a few of his followers on the appointed date and place, and nothing happened. His power was destroyed. There was a whispered rumor that he simply vanished, or that he had been eaten by his two black wolves. Few wanted to even wonder, or to speak his name.

Now, as I have said, that first day was a dreadful, fearful time. But life goes on. I was trying to benefit from some of this new wisdom. I know one thing for sure. I paid more attention to the seriousness of my morning ritual. My cleansing and my prayers at daybreak each day took on a far more serious tone. No longer were the songs merely something to do to fulfill a duty. They began to take on meaning.

Yes, I see some with more life experience smiling and nodding. You were right, when you probably shook your heads in despair sometimes at my lack of understanding. Does not each of us go through a time when parents and maybe all adults, know nothing about anything? Ah, I see more nods.

Most young people come to see the error of their ways. Usually, slowly. Sometimes it takes much longer than for others. But a big danger, if the young person survives it, speeds the whole learning process somehow. His parents increase in wisdom very quickly, in his mind. Ah, I see some nodding of heads. You have been there, too?

I cannot remember when the next big quake happened. There were so many, over so long a time. We lost count. No one could even count the small tremors, but there were enough big ones... I am getting ahead of my story, though.

I mentioned the waterspout that someone claimed to have seen. Many did not believe him. As it turned out, water was one of our biggest dangers in the moons ahead. Water is supposed to flow downhill, no? But what is to happen when the hill moves?

We had seen some of the hillside slide down into the ravine, and the water of the blocked stream beginning to rise. There were also places in the flat prairie that seemed to sink, leaving a low spot, maybe the distance of a bow shot across. How deep? It was hard to tell, but maybe more than the height of a man. Yes, it is true! The odd thing; such a low spot, even in our Tallgrass Hills, would be wet. There would be a shallow pond, with ducks, other water birds, and water plants. It was unreal, to see such a lowland that was completely dry. But we had only to wait! It would fill.

I should add... As if to balance the falling of that area, we realized some time later that there were other places that were pushed. You can see that we began to distrust our own eyes. A tree, or knoll or hill where we had looked up to see it, now we would often be looking down on a treetop, that of a tree maybe three or four times the height of a man.

Many of those who were there were very frightened. Everyone was having a hard time staying on their feet. It was easy to lose balance, with the solid outlines of surrounding trees and hills and even the horizon appearing to move, like the shimmer of the distant hills in the heat of summer.

Oh, yes... The young husband who blundered into the hornets' nest died the next day. The swelling closed off his breathing. We never learned what had happened to the horse.

CHAPTER THIRTEEN

From about this time in my story, things begin to blur together. It is hard to remember, even now, which things came first, and which, after that. Nothing seemed to make any sense at all. There were those who were sure that the world was ending. Not about to end, you see, but that it had already begun.

The whites, especially, seemed to have more trouble with this. I had not seen many whites before. Most of those were trappers or mountain men who are more like we are. Most of them have "Indian" wives, or none at all. It is strange, to realize that I had never seen a white woman until that time. That alone was a great surprise.

Why, you ask? *Aiee*, you would have to see it, to understand. Did you know that white women cannot even own any property? All they have belongs to their husbands. Our women would never consent to such things as these women do.

For instance, there is no place for a woman to go when her moon time comes. It is known that it may be dangerous for her to be around the lodge at this time. If she should accidentally touch a weapon, maybe her husband's bow, during her moon time, it may never shoot straight again. The safest thing for her to do is to move into the Moon Lodge for the few days that it lasts. This relieves her of responsibilities during that time, when she may be dangerous anyway.

Whites seem not to understand this. Their women are not honored and respected enough to allow them this short escape each moon, until her moon time is past, and she can return to her family, rested and ready to be welcomed home.

But, no, stop with the questions. This is part of the story, but let me tell it. I only learned a little at a time.

I was proud of White Plume during those early days of the shaking earth. She was steady and brave, and I was reminded of the "manly-hearted" women in our stories of the People. This is something that we have always prized in our history. Our women are strong and brave.

Remember Running Eagle, who became a warrior long ago by earning that privilege. Or, Pale Star, kidnapped as a child, making her way home as the wife of one of the Francois. Even Bear's Rump, who saved her husband by jabbing the spear that he had dropped, into the rear end of the bear that was mauling him.

But, as I saw the white women, I realized that they are different from ours. Yes, they have some strong ones, but most are content to obey their husbands. Maybe "content" is not the way to explain it. But they seem to think it normal, not being able to speak in council, or to vote when a decision is being made.

I did not find them very attractive anyway, with their pale skins and watery eyes of blue or green. Some, even young ones, looked to me like persons who had been sick a long time. To me, not a white woman I have seen was as attractive as our women, with some color in their cheeks.

Some of them seem sad all the time, unable to face any ordinary trouble at all, even. There was one we encountered who was terrified, over every bit of misfortune, afraid of everything. There were, of course, many causes to be afraid.

One of the greatest dangers was that everything seemed to have been shaken out of place by the squirming of the earth. It did not help that this was the Moon of Long Nights, with Sun Boy's torch fading anyway. Maybe this was a sign. In all the history of the People, there have been the stories about this. Jokes, even: What if Sun Boy's torch goes out, and is not renewed? He always relights a new torch, but what if, this time... Well, it is easy to see that this was nothing to joke about.

I was in a situation where there were hardly any people who were ours, the People. I had no one who knew our own stories and customs. I have to admit that it was a very frightening thing. Lone Fox was a big help, because in their travels, Fox had become familiar with many tribes and nations, and with their stories and customs. That was good because the reactions differed widely. Some were sure that this was truly the end of the world, as I said. Others related it to some of their own stories. There were Osages and Miss-ouree and Cherokee, and many others, I suppose. I told about Tsali, the prophet, and of Tecumseh, who had predicted that the earth would shake. There was much nodding of heads and telling of "I remember when..." among the elders. That soon stopped, because it was quickly seen that no one alive had seen or even heard of such a thing as this. There was nothing to compare, not only in the lifetimes of people in that area, but anywhere. Even in the oldest stories of any other people we talked to, even in their Creation stories there was nothing like this. That was not reassuring. If no one from this wide mix of many tribes had ever seen or heard of such happenings, what chance did we have? We could not even run, because we didn't know where. In any direction, it might be even worse.

There were some who would have blamed it on the whites, but that was not a very convincing argument. There were many whites, and they were in as much danger as anyone.

I mentioned that an old woman had been killed when her house fell in. That was a white woman, I heard, but did not see it happen, or see the body. Whites mostly bury the dead in the ground, it seems.

Among all of the people we saw, there were those, both the natives and whites, who seemed to go mad with fear. Others went calmly about, looking after the needs of themselves and their families. What else could we do? Whatever was to happen, there were some needs that could not be avoided. Food, water, and shelter of some sort had to come first in any planning that anyone could do.

I had already mentioned our makeshift shelter. It could be improved upon, which we did, day by day. Food was not immediately a problem, because we had dried meat and pemmican. There were springs for water, which seemed not to be affected much yet. Later, it was another story.

I had told, I think, about the actions of the animals? Even before that first shock the dogs had seemed restless. Horses, too. I am made to think that animals have a feel for such things. We know that when the swallows hunt the insects that fly close to the ground, it means rain will come soon. How do they know?

But that is another matter. What I want to tell is more serious. The Moon of Madness affects the deer, as we know, but that happens every year, and is soon over. We expect it, even use it as we prepare for winter. But now! *Aiee!*

Here is an example: We, the People, do not kill bears. We have little contact with them in the Tallgrass Hills anyway, except for the Real-bears who follow the buffalo herds, looking for an occasional kill. We let them alone, and they do the same for us, from our covenant at Creation. Most of other tribes and nations do not have a covenant with Bear. Some hunt him to eat, and for his heavy fur. Whites like to hunt him for both. Bear and his habits are well known to us, even as we avoid trouble by avoiding him. In the Moon of Ripening, and that of

Falling Leaves, Bear begins to fatten himself with nuts and acorns. He needs to be fat so that he can disappear into some cave or a tangle of fallen trees and brush to sleep all winter. We almost never see him until the Moon of Awakening. If he is roused accidentally before that time, he is very bad-natured. Was there not one of our own Northern band who was named "Winter Bear" because of his angry disposition? You understand the idea.

Now, think of the conditions where I was, with Lone Fox and his family. Every few days, it seemed, there would be another shock, or two or three, big enough to startle us. Big enough, in fact, to wake the winter bears.

There are many bears in that part of the world. Mostly, the black bears, smaller than the Real-bears that follow the herds, but big enough! More than enough. Bigger than a man, and in evil temper from having been rolled from their sleep by the shaking earth.

That was only a part of the danger. In such a situation, in any time of trouble, I suppose, it brings out the best in any person. Or maybe the worst. We saw both. I have thought deeply about this, and I have come to think that what danger brings out in anyone is only that which is in him already. Could it be otherwise? It is like testing a new bow. If it has a flaw, it will be discovered, but so will an unexpected strength, or weakness. It is much like trying a new horse.

Yes, forgive me. I will get on with my story. But it has caused me to do much thinking, which is important to the story, too.

CHAPTER FOURTEEN

It had been a few days since the first quaking of the ground, when the hillside collapsed. There were some trembles from time to time, but with each one, we were a little less afraid. Maybe, as some thought, the trembles were growing smaller. Some children even found them amusing as they became a familiar part of each day. Toad was one of those. I have said that he was different, and that the whole disaster was bringing out the true nature of everyone. He was one of those who seemed to enjoy each tremor, and the effort to stay standing.

Unless you have felt it, there is no way to understand. You are just ready to put a foot down, and the spot where you intended to put it is not there, but further to the left, or further ahead. It is much like being on a half-trained, skittish horse, except that you are not sitting, but standing, on its moving back. It is easy to fall.

I don't remember exactly how long it may have been since the first shocks. It does not really matter, I suppose. Yet after all we had already experienced, it came as a complete surprise.

There was a tremor that struck and continued to rumble. I had left our shelter and was gathering firewood. As I have said, that was one of our biggest problems. It was a sunny day, but at that season Sun Boy's torch is none too warm at its best. We needed the fuel. There were others in the woods, too, all for the same purpose. Or possibly, hunting rabbits or squirrels.

That tremor was a complete surprise to me in its power. You cannot, unless you have felt it yourself, imagine the sensation.

A woman nearby, maybe a stone's throw from me in a little clearing, hesitated for the space of a few heartbeats. Then she screamed, a long, earsplitting wail, like the hunting scream of the big long-tailed cat. It caused the hair on the back of my neck to stand up. Then, after she stopped a moment to take a deep breath, she tossed her entire armful of firewood into the air and ran, crashing through the brush, going who knows where, screaming all the way.

I was beginning to notice the different ways that people were reacting to this time of madness. That was one way. This was not a white woman, you understand, but a native wife of one of the trappers. I had not realized until about that time, that the big differences in people are not which tribe or nation, or whether white or native, or even black. Yes, I had heard of black white men. Fox told me that they are usually slaves of white men. At first, some thought that they were men who were painted that way for making medicine, a special dance ceremony, maybe. But this medicine paint does not come off. The skin has that color. I do not know if it ever comes off. I have heard from others who have seen the black white men wash in the river, as we do, and they said that their color is unchanged. I was told later that some of these, slaves of the other white men, maybe, had run away and were living with some of the tribes in the Ar-kansa.

But, back to my story... It was that day, I think, that I began to see the differences in the ways people behave in bad times. There was that woman, who tossed her fuel and seemed to go mad. Others, who have seemed foolish and unreliable, may prove to be the strongest in a time of trouble.

And that, my friends, was a day of trouble. I had just begun to think that this new rumble was quieting down, when it began again, stronger than before. An open, grassy meadow that I could see through the trees, seeming to drop away, for maybe the height of a man. That sinking appearance, starting about two or three bow shots to the east, came toward me in a wave, like water blown by wind, but falling instead of rising. Some good-sized trees swayed and fell. The solid ground dropped out from under me, and I fell, too, hitting the ground hard enough to knock the wind from my lungs. My firewood scattered, as I squirmed around, trying to catch my breath. Three deer crashed past me in the underbrush, completely panicked, and headed out into the clearing.

Just then I was horrified to see a spurt of water shoot up out of the very ground that had dropped away. It was hard to tell how big or how high this was, because there was no familiar object near by. As nearly as I can recall, it was maybe a long bow shot from me, and the stream of water about as big around as the trunk of a tree. A tree that I could circle with my arms. Its power, though, pushed water straight up, higher than the tallest trees in that area. Much water.

I had heard, from Fox and other traders, of the places far west of our country, where these waterspouts blow up into the air at regular times. But, I had thought that in that country, there are also boiling springs, where they could cook the fish they catch. The waterspouts are hot. I was afraid, and one of my fears was that this waterspout would be boiling, and would fill the valley with a scalding bath. I had no desire to be scalded to death.

As I caught my breath and scrambled to my feet, I began to realize that although it was a frosty day, the waterspout was not steaming. So, it was not hot, but cold. True, I knew very little about such things, but even then, it seemed unusual to me. Everything, the whole world, was being turned upside down and inside out. And yes, I was wishing sometimes that I was back in my mother's lodge.

I stood staring, looking at that rush of water into the air. It was so big a stream that I began to wonder how long it would take to fill the just-formed basin below me. Not really below me, I quickly realized.

I was actually in the basin, though near its rim, as nearly as I could tell.

When a creek bed is dry, it is very hard to guess where its high water mark will be when the rain comes. This was a similar thing, but with none of the signs of previous high water that we can usually see. It was completely a guess, and the ground was still rumbling. It could rise or fall again at any moment, and I felt a need to get away from that place.

I gathered up part of my spilled firewood, and hurried back toward our camp. I had some difficulty in finding my way, because some familiar landmarks had changed. A giant old sycamore which had once marked the bend of the creek now lay across and partly in the creek. Other trees were down. The rumbling continued.

I was nearly knocked down by a horse that came pounding past me, running in a blind panic, running to escape the terrible fear of a horror it could not understand.

Aside from my own fear, I had now regained my senses to a point where it suddenly struck me: Where is White Plume? Is she safe?

Looking back, that may have been a turning point, when I was no longer worried for myself, but for another, a loved one.

I reached our camp. A tree had fallen, its top branches partially hiding the lean-to. Dove was standing by the fire, looking at the fallen tree, not moving. There were still rumblings beneath our feet.

Dove turned to look at me, eyes wide.

"Where are the others?" I asked her.

"Fox and Toad went to chop browse for the horses," she said.

"Where is White Plume?" I asked quickly.

Dove's eyes widened even more.

"I... I thought she was with you!"

Moon of Madness

CHAPTER FIFTEEN

I felt at that moment, much as I did when I was small and was kicked in the stomach by a young colt. It was an accident, a playful kick as the animal raced around and around where my father was grooming the colt's mother.

I had been playing with her foal, maybe half a moon of age, running and dodging. It was a big colt, one which was to make a buffalo runner when it was grown. It did not try to hurt me, I think, but kicked out as it ran past. I tried to grab at it, which was a mistake. The colt struck out with both hind feet, as they do when playing with each other. One hoof missed me, just barely brushing past my side. The other caught me in the soft part just below where the ribs come together at the middle. I fell.

I could not draw breath, and lay there gasping like a fish out of water, my father said later.

What? Oh, yes. I know that is not part of my story. But, that was how I felt when Dove told me about White Plume. I had gone to gather wood, and Fox and Toad to look after horses. In winter, there, whites sometimes feed dry grass, cut in summer for the purpose. "Hay," it is called. Some of the natives do this too, but Fox, from the plains, fed horses more as the People do.

We would cut small sticks from the cottonwood trees to add to the standing dry grass the horses could graze.

Fox had told Dove where they were going, and since White Plume was nowhere to be seen, they assumed that she was with me.

Now, this might be a bad thing. White Plume, though I always thought her soft and warm, was hard, too. Like her namesake, she was equipped with a set of claws. She had grown up, learning to defend herself and to fight when necessary. Our women are not to be considered weak, and neither was this one.

On the other hand, this was a town which was mostly whites, and many of them are not to be trusted. This could be a bad situation.

By the time Fox and Toad returned to our camp, Dove and I had asked several of our closest neighbors whether they had seen the girl. We asked a white trapper and his wife, the one who had panicked in the woods. She was better now. The husband, who had been at home in their lodge, had seen or heard nothing unusual. At least, until the quake struck again.

A white family, in one of the square log houses a little farther away, seemed annoyed that we would bother them. Maybe they were afraid of us.

"Girl not here! Go away!"

This, in spite of the fact that Dove had a pretty good use of the Yen-glees tongue. She had done the asking.

Fox, with his trader's skills, and with the contacts he had made since we arrived, was no more successful than Dove and I. Several people remembered her, but had not seen her that day.

"Maybe this morning... No, that was yesterday..."

Our quest came up empty.

"A person does not just disappear!" insisted Dove.

"Someone must have seen something."

It did not help that everyone had spent most of that day worrying about the earthquake, and trying to repair their own damage.

Shadows were growing long when we found an old woman who gave us some possible help. A couple of trappers who had been camped about a bow-shot from her house had passed earlier, but after the quake had quieted. They seemed to have two pack horses, she recalled, and a third person with them whom she had not seen before. All three were bundled against the winter cold, but this one, a little shorter than the others, may have been a woman. She recalled that she had not seen a wife around their camp, and thought it odd.

"Were these white men?" asked Fox quickly.

"I am not sure," the woman apologized. "Many trappers look alike and dress alike."

"Thank you, Mother," Fox said as we turned to go. "Oh, yes, which way did they go?"

"That way," she pointed to one of the paths which led to the south and east.

"Do you know what is that way?" I asked Fox as we left.

"The Big River, the Missi-sippi," he said. "Maybe a day's travel from here. It loops around some. Maybe closer."

"There is a trail going that way," Dove noted.

"Yes," agreed Fox, "but it grows dark. Let us look at their camp first."

It was very dark before we finished looking at the camp site that the trappers had just left. It had little to show us, except that they were not very neat in habit.

"One or both are white men," Fox observed. "Big fire." He pointed to the large amount of ash where their fire had been.

"A white man builds a big fire and can't get close enough to keep warm. An Indian warms, close to a small fire. Probably, both white."

I was tempted to try to convince Fox to start in pursuit, but realized it would be foolish. We could not travel a strange trail, or even trail, with winter darkness upon us. We hurried back to our camp, and Fox explained the situation to his wife.

"I will start as soon as it is light enough to see the trail," he told her. "You three stay here."

I was completely surprised, as I had expected to go with Fox. Now, I would have to be very convincing.

"Uncle," I began seriously, "I may have done some childish things, but you know that I have learned much. I have not done anything foolish for some time, and I have worked hard. You have probably seen my love for your daughter, and guessed that my wish is to marry her. She is in danger, and you cannot fight two men alone. I deserve a chance to help the woman I love, and I will do whatever you say."

Toad giggled, his mother gasped, and Fox sat, staring into the fire for a long time.

Finally he spoke, his voice sounding tired and old. I had never heard him sound like this.

"You are right, Badger. I do need help."

He turned and spoke to Toad.

"Toad, your foolishness is over. You will stay with your mother, and you will do what she says, or answer to me. Show your mother where we cut browse for the horses. You two will have to do it tomorrow. Maybe it will take us only a day or two."

Dove was crying.

"We will take care of them," she said.

"I know," Fox assured her.

We were up, a few supplies packed, and ready to saddle the horses by the time the gray in the east began to fade to yellow. As it became lighter, we went to where the horses were kept, not far away, and prepared to leave.

"I don't see Rabbit Horse," said Fox to Toad. "He's probably untied his tether. Better find him this morning."

Toad nodded obediently. I felt more confident about the boy now. Maybe he would learn from this experience. Rabbit Horse, the mule, had been noted for his strange habits, one of which was to untie the rope that fastened him to a tree or rock. I sincerely hoped that this experience would make a man out of the never-serious youngster. I felt assured that had never been as immature and unreasonable as Toad, though now... But, let me go on.

I had thought that we would surely catch up with the trappers by noon. Noon came and went, and we had seen no one on the trail. Could we have taken a wrong trail? We could not see how. Their pack horses could not travel as fast as our riding horses, and we should have seen some signs. What now?

"Something is wrong," Fox said. "They have taken a side trail, somewhere."

We had found no tracks, so we retraced the trail, back almost to the town, where there were many hoofprints. Finally we noticed a narrow trail, branching off in a more easterly direction, where the main trail headed south. There were tracks, of two horses, as the woman had described back at the town.

We had wasted most of the morning, and part of the afternoon. We hurried to follow this new trail, knowing that there was no way that we could overtake them before night. When darkness fell, we made a dry camp, with only a small fire to break the chill of the Moon of Long Nights.

That chill was nothing, compared to the chill in my heart as I thought of White Plume's situation. I did not sleep very much, and my heart was very heavy.

CHAPTER SIXTEEN

I have not told you much of White Plume, except that I was struck with her beauty and her charm. I now have to admit that my attraction to her was a very childish thing, when I left my parents' lodge. Still, White Plume and I, while it may have been a childish attraction at first, had grown closer in the time since. I believe that what we felt toward each other had grown, and was more realistic, more grown-up.

It had become so during the time that she had helped to bring me back to health when I had been battered by the buck's antlers. She had seen me at my worst, and still had serious and adult feelings toward me.

In addition to my gratitude for her help, I continued to gain respect and admiration for her. She had a sense of humor, and was amusing to be with. She could find fun in the worst of situations. In truth, that had been one of my problems while I was recovering. She would catch me unsuspecting, with some remark that made me laugh, which would drive a spear of pain through my battered ribs. Then, she would feel sorrow, which would make my heart heavy for her, and I would apologize, making her giggle, and... Well, you can see some of our problems.

But that had been long ago, it seemed. We had become close friends, in addition to our attraction to each other. I have come to think that this is the best way. Friends first, before becoming lovers. We had not yet come to a point where we could be considered lovers, but when White Plume was missing, only then did I begin to fully understand the depth of my feeling for her.

Now, because White Plume is not here, I will try to tell you what we learned later about that day that she dis-appeared. This is very hard for me, as you can understand.

White Plume had been helping her mother with the camp chores, and had been looking for firewood near by, when the first tremor of that morning struck. There were enough houses and tents close by, that there was much noise and confusion. White Plume started back toward our camp, but came upon a small child who had been struck by a falling tree. He was crying, blood smeared down the side of his face.

"Where is your mother?" she asked.

The boy pointed in a general direction, but stood still, yelling.

"Can you walk?" she asked him.

The child, maybe three or four summers old, nodded but made no effort to do so. White Plume's mothering instinct overcame her judgment.

"Come, I'll help you," she said, taking the boy's hand. "Which way?"

It seemed later that the child must have been confused, pointing one way and then another. White Plume, having started the task of finding the child's family, had no choice now. She could not abandon him. This led her farther from our camp, and into new surroundings.

When she finally was able to restore the child to a grateful and tearful mother, she started back toward more familiar territory.

I do not know the exact details of what happened next. White Plume had started back to our camp when she was stopped by a man she had seen before, around the town. He was a trapper, by his appearance. My heart is heavy when I think of it.

I do not know whether she might have screamed. I am sure that she must have fought. But there was apparently no one to see the attack. Yet, with all of the earth tremors that were happening nearly every day, a scream was not unusual. I have just told of a woman who screamed, threw down her firewood and ran. In that time of madness, a scream of distress had lost its meaning.

I have many times placed guilt on myself over this. I told myself that it was my fault. I should have been with her. I could imagine the worst, what this man and his partner might do to the woman I loved. There were times when I wanted to scream out, in my own agony. This was a very bad time, worse than any in my life. I could not sleep, wondering and worrying about White Plume. A time or two, I thought of starting on along the trail. Each time I rejected the thought. Not only was it too dark a night, but a chilling cold, as well. That had been the weather pattern, warming some during the day, and freezing each night.

The main thought that prevented me from doing something completely foolish, however, was my pledge to Lone Fox. I had promised to do as he said, and if I had done anything foolish, it would forever be a festering sore between us. I must take no risks, and also remember that any stupid act on my part could easily cause the death of the woman I loved.

I actually dozed off for a little while, toward morning. I woke in a panic, brought on by a terrible dream in which the two trappers were abusing and assaulting White Plume. Fox was rekindling the fire, adding dry twigs to the hot coals, all that remained of our night fire. As it broke into a flame, he tossed a pinch of tobacco into the hottest part, to appease the local spirits.

"But we are moving on," I blurted.

"True," said the trader. "But the spirits enjoy the taste of tobacco. Besides, maybe they can travel, as we do. Maybe they have spirit-friends where we are going, and Badger... You know that we will need any and all help that we can find."

He looked old and tired, and my heart was heavy for him, too. This steadied me some. I must not fail him, either. By the first light of dawn, we were on the move, cautiously, of course.

We found their campsite as the sun rose a little higher, and began to identify certain tracks. Three persons... One man wore the hard boots of a white man, another the softer moccasin of the southern plains, with a rawhide sole. This meant nothing as far as identification. Trappers might adopt any tribe's customs. But a third track, slender and feminine, told us that White Plume was still alive.

There was one other sign, one that could easily have been overlooked. I might have missed it, but Fox called attention to it; a broken twig on a shrub near the now dead campfire. It seems insignificant now, but at the time, the most important discovery ever.

The twig was bent and broken upward, yet dangled on a narrow strip of bark. If it had been broken by a browsing deer, it would have been chewed and frayed. If a man had broken it, especially a white man, he would most likely bend it downward, and break it off, rather than leave it to dangle.

"White Plume has left us a sign," Fox explained. "She knows we will follow, and wants us to know she is alive and able to think and plan."

This was a great comfort. It did not make the situation any better, but it did provide hope. We would have to be alert, watching for the next message that White Plume might be able to leave for us.

We had no idea how far ahead of us the other party might be. We had by this time begun to identify some of the horse tracks. One of their horses seemed to "paddle" a little on the left front foot, the twist scuffing up the dirt as the hoof lifted each time. We saw no tracks of other travelers, as far as we could tell. The only fresh tracks were those of the ones we were following.

The animal with the odd paddling gait on the left was probably a pack horse. Such a defect would not be a limitation for a pack horse, but might be rejected for riding purposes. It would be so among the People, anyway. There was no way to tell what a white man would think. You know how they are.

The fourth, another pack animal, had a different shaped foot. This track was not round, like that of most horses, but narrower on the sides, rounded on the front. Probably a pack animal, maybe a donkey.

That came to four, the animals whose tracks we had begun to recognize. Two were probably pack animals, we thought. Except for the footprints at their night camp, we saw none that indicated anyone on foot. They would be traveling faster this way, so we must keep moving.

We decided, since there seemed to be no footprints of people, except at their camp, that White Plume must be riding one of the pack animals. If, of course, she was still alive. We dared not think otherwise.

Looking back, it was very fortunate that we were not fighting a hard winter. Yes, it was hard, of course, but the weather, I mean. If the snow had been as heavy as it is in some years, we might have had even more trouble to deal with. As it was, the springs and small streams were crusted with ice each morning, thawing during the day and frosting again each night. It could have been worse, though at the time I could scarcely imagine that anything could be worse. It was a terrible experience, trying to catch up to the men who had taken White Plume. Our pace was slowed by the fact that we must stop frequently to look for tracks and to be certain that they had not taken one of the dim trails that branched off.

Fox also insisted that we stop to examine every place that they had paused to dismount. At first I did not understand this approach. He finally explained. Only then, by looking for her tracks could we be certain that White Plume was still alive and able to walk. We had no way, otherwise, and very little knowledge of how she was being treated. I was just beginning to realize how dangerous her situation was. At any time her captors might decide that she was too much trouble. They might kill her, if she proved to become a problem to their travel.

We had no way to guess what indignities she might have been subjected to. I did not even want to think of it, but was forced to look at her plight realistically. For what purpose might two men want to abduct an attractive young woman? Aside from the immediate satisfaction of their own animal urges, it was possible that they might choose to sell her. Oddly, Fox, with his trader's approach, saw this as a good thing. As long as she represented a value for sale or trade, her captors would probably keep her alive. As you might expect, I was somewhat less than pleased at this theory, though I had to admit that it was probably true. The irritation that I felt over Fox's attitude faded quickly, as I realized that he was right. He, too, was suffering at the thoughts of what might be happening to the young woman we both loved.

And, much as either of us hated to think of it, the kidnapers had a reason to treat their captive well. Any severe abuse might lessen the trade value of a young woman. We did not speak much of this, but both of us were strongly feeling it as we traveled on, following the dim trail.

Chapter Seventeen

We were not making any progress. We would travel, camp at dark, get up and follow the tracks again. We did not seem to be gaining any. Those we followed were always a day's travel ahead.

I do not know how many days we did this. Only a few, probably, but it seemed endless to me. To Fox, too, I am sure, but he talked little.

There were sometimes a few tremors, in strength from a tiny quiver under us to jarring rumbles that caused panic to the animals. Fortunately, our horses were steady and experienced on the trail.

The area where we were is a mix of grassland and heavy timber, with thickets of scrub oak and other small trees in between. There were many pines, too, still green in winter. I have come to think that I am more suited to open prairie. It was hard, not to be able to see more than a bowshot ahead, in many places.

Almost every new line of sight brought surprises, the results of the quakes. In places, the earth had moved enough to block the trail. Still animals, and probably people, had found their way around newly formed ponds and fallen stands of timber. You can imagine how much more difficult it was to be sure we were on the right trail.

In one place, a grove of pines stood with only the tops showing above water level. A whole area, maybe several bow-shots across, had dropped enough to form a small lake.

Half a day's travel beyond that, we came to an open space maybe twice that size, where nothing was growing at all. It was covered with mud, and dead fish were scattered along the entire valley. Many crows and a few eagles were busily fighting over this feast, though there was plenty for all. At one place, a family of coyotes had marked their camp, and were chasing off any intruders. In another, a lone badger held his ground. There were many tracks of raccoons, badger, and other scavengers everywhere in the field of icy mud. It took a few moments to understand that this had been a lake, now dry because the whole section of earth had been thrust upward. Its water had filled, maybe, the grove of trees we had seen flooded the day before. Or maybe, that had been another lake or river.

This whole thing was very confusing. It would have been easy to go completely mad, worrying about it. Usually when we travel, especially on the prairie, we can see a ridge, a valley, a river or stream, a day's travel ahead. In the Tallgrass Hills, the People often choose the camp site for tomorrow night when traveling, no?

We can see ahead. But here, with the ground rising or falling, today's lake might be a hilltop tomorrow, and the hilltop under water.

Somewhere ahead, Fox said, there should be a river.

"You have been here before?" I asked him.

"Not exactly where we are," he answered. "The general area. You see, Badger, this area has much more water than most of the range of your people. There are springs and streams, and many that come together and form rivers that flow into the Big River, the Miss-iss-ippi. I am made to think that it may be somewhere near, but I am not sure. When the earth itself is squirming like a nest of maggots on a rotting carcass, who knows what will happen next?"

I had never seen Fox in this much doubt, and it was not a good thing. Still, how could he think otherwise?

We came to a small settlement, a town mostly of whites, with the usual mix of others. Here might be a chance to ask about the party we were trailing. Maybe, even, they might still be here. We must be careful, though. We had no idea whether the trappers we were trailing might have friends here.

"We have to think on this," said Fox. "We don't know whether they know they are followed."

"But White Plume knows," I reminded. "She may leave signs."

"Yes... Let us think on this, Badger. Would they know us when they see us?"

We could not decide. We were looking for two men dressed like trappers, probably both white, but not for sure. We had at best, a second hand description of the men. As to whether they might have seen us back at the other town, we had no way of knowing.

Fox was glancing at the sky, which was becoming overcast. "Snow, maybe," he muttered, half to himself.

It was only a little past mid-day, and experienced travelers like those we followed would probably not move on in the face of an impending storm. They would camp.

Fox had reached the same conclusion. "They'll camp. Maybe, even, this is their home."

I had not thought of that. Still, even white trappers might have homes.

"Let us make camp," he went on. "Then we can walk around and see what we can. Even if they think they're followed they will not start on, this close to night. They probably do not know us, anyway."

"It is good," I agreed.

We found a place to camp, and, with dark coming on, quickly made a small lean-to of brush and a canvas. Fox insisted that we start a camp fire.

"Not to do so would attract attention," he reminded.

It was true, of course.

He sprinkled the necessary pinch of tobacco to honor the spirits of the place, and we tethered the horses.

"Now, let us separate," he suggested. "Just wander around. If you see them, try not to go any closer. They may not even know what we look like, but we don't want to warn them. See what we can, and be back here before dark. If you see White Plume, pretend not to notice. Get away as quick as you can."

We decided to circle the settlement, walking in opposite directions. We would probably meet at some point on the other side. If not, we would continue the circle and meet back at our campfire. We would avoid contact with the trappers if we did find them until we had a chance to plan our attack.

The settlement was larger than we thought. It was also strung out along the river, making it long and narrow. I quickly came to see that our plan to meet on the other side of the settlement was not a good one. But, no matter. We would meet back at the camp. Fox's plan was good.

Still, darkness was falling quickly, as it does in winter. I was beginning to wonder if I could find my way back to the camp. The moon was a few days before full, and might give some light, except for the thin, cloudy overcast, and the threat of snow.

I was half tempted to change my agreed-upon plan and return to our camp the way I had come, when I saw Fox, a stone's throw ahead. He was standing on a low hill or ridge, facing east. He seemed to be completely motionless, just standing and staring. He did not even turn as I approached, which was unusual in itself. He should have been more concerned when someone approached from behind him.

As I came up the little rise to where he stood, I realized that he was staring at the river. We had talked, that the river should be ahead, the Miss-iss-ippi or one of the other rivers which join it in this area. I was not prepared, though, for what I saw. From where we stood, there was nothing but water stretching into the distance. It was growing dark, of course, but to be unable to see the other side of the river was a shock to my inexperienced senses.

I glanced at Fox, and was puzzled, that he seemed as impressed and confused as I was. Had he not seen the Big River before? Yes, he had described it to me.

Now I had seen lakes and marshes of considerable size before, some large enough that the distant shore was really distant. I could accept the fact that near nightfall I might not be able to see the other bank of the Big River in the dusk. That was not the surprise for me, but that there was an active, flowing current in the stream, running from my right to left, carrying bits of floating trash, as any river will. The thing that puzzled me was Fox's fascination with it.

"Uncle," I spoke to him, "what is it? You have seen the Big River before, no?"

He turned, and there was a blank, empty look in his eyes. It took a little while for the blank look in his eyes to settle on my face.

"Badger," he finally said in a hushed voice, "there is something very wrong."

"What is wrong?" I asked, confused.

"We know that the Big River runs to the south, no?"

"That is what I have heard," I told him.

"There are twists and bends to any stream," he went on dreamily. "I have seen this river, before, and it does so, too. But look, Badger. We are facing east..."

I began to see what he was trying to say.

The current was carrying the floating sticks and leaves from our right to the left. The river was flowing northward.

"Badger," he said, "the Big River is flowing backward. Is this the end of the world, backward to Creation?"

I had never seen Fox like this. In everything that had happened, he had never seemed to lose the confidence that I admired in him. That had been maybe the most powerful attraction to his family, for me. Well, you chuckle... Of course, I was with them because I had been smitten by the charms of his daughter, White Plume. It was that, yes, the beginning of my connection to the family.

But it had quickly become much more. Through the time I had been with them, much had changed. I had come to see the parents of White Plume as family, and they had accepted me. I was still unsure about Toad, but what is to be done about a boy of that age, anyway? They cannot be told anything, especially by their own parents. Their judgment is always in question, and often they cannot be trusted. I pause to mention these things, because I, myself, at the time was barely growing out from under the influence of the same handicaps in my own life. But, we are never aware of it at the time. Only as we look back can we see ourselves as we were, and feel the shame and embarrassment which escaped us at the time.

I am trying to let you know how I felt, then. During the time when our own parents seem to know nothing, we come to admire the wisdom of another. Sometimes we even begin to learn. Only later do we realize that all parents gain much in wisdom during these years.

It was at that place in my life. I had never seen Fox in a situation where he seemed to have any doubt as to what should be done. I had come to think of him as one who would always have the wisdom, the insight, the knowledge, and the strength to do whatever became necessary.

You can see, then, what a helpless feeling came over me when I saw Fox staring at the river in complete confusion. Always before, no matter how bad the situation, Fox had been able to see a plan of action of some sort. Even when White Plume disappeared, he had instantly begun to form plans to recover her. I had come to expect his wisdom to find a way to handle anything that might happen, and had never doubted him.

Now, here he stood, helplessly watching the Big River run backwards into time. Or, was it Time itself that had reached a point where it had become fully wound, and must reverse?

There came to my mind a memory of watching a craftsman use a bow drill, to make a hole in a shell he was working. He would wind the rawhide thong around the spindle of the tool, and place the cutting tip of the flint in the exact spot he wanted. A firm push downward on the bar would set the spindle to whirling as the thong unwound, reversed, and rewound in the opposite direction. Another push, another whirl, again and again, each stroke cutting deeper into the shell, finally breaking through, a hole through which a sinew could be tied, and the shell ornament became a pendant.

I felt stupid even at the time as I watched the river flow backward. Fox's self-questioning about the meaning of the world came down hard. I could see his feeling, as I remembered the whir of the bow drill. Wind, whirl, stop, reverse, rewind, again, again... The world's time interval would be so long that even the Creation story might not contain it.

Do the rivers run until the end of time, and then, in a maddening series of quakes and trembling, stop and rewind, like the drill's thong, reversing direction and starting over? It appeared to be happening, as the evening darkness deepened, and the river ran upstream.

What would happen next? A strange thought flapped through my head, like the wingbeat of a vulture attempting to rise above carrion, gorged with its rotting repast.

The pale, winter sun was just setting in the west. Where would it rise? Would it go on around, as it always has in human experience, or would it pause, rewind, and rise in the west now, with the reversal of Creation? Or, were we all going mad?

CHAPTER EIGHTEEN

We hurried back to our own camp in the deepening dark-ness. I was concerned over Fox's quiet.

I built the fire up, and began to take out some jerky. No matter what, we should eat. I was unsure what to say, so I said nothing.

It was apparent that neither of us had discovered any trace of the trappers or the missing White Plume. My heart was very heavy over this, but what could I do, in strange country, with the leader's wisdom on which I had depended now unavailable to me?

Fox sat across the campfire, mumbling softly to himself, and not even appearing to notice me. A little at a time, I began to understand that I had a real problem. In spite of my boastful confidence when I left my parents' lodge, I now realized that I had not been ready for such a quest as this. After my injury, it had been easy to be humble. I had been able to accept, in a childish way, that I was really quite dependent on the experience of the trader. I respected Fox's wisdom in this. He had been thoughtful enough not to call attention to my childish weaknesses. I seldom thought about it, though his approval was always a thing of great value to me. I was learning a great many things, largely due to his wisdom and his patience with me.

You can imagine, then, my feelings as I sat across our small campfire from Fox that night. Only now did I begin to see how much I really needed his strength. I had used the benefits of his experience with little appreciation or thanks.

Now, when I desperately needed this wisdom, it seemed that he was out of reach. It was as if Fox had somehow departed his body. It was not like the expected event that occurs at death, with the spirit moving out to cross over to the Other Side, as a part of the Great Mystery. Even that would have been easier to understand, I felt.

But Fox sat, mumbling to himself, staring blankly... I tell you, my friends, this was a bad time. His spirit, on which the survival of both of us would have to depend, was off wandering along the backward-flowing river somewhere. His suggestion that time was flowing backward to rewind itself became more and more alarming. Was I to grow younger and more helpless as time slipped backward?

I tried to think calmly. What would Fox do, if he was able to do something? I must think...

He would tend the fire. Yes, I had already done that. I tossed another stick on the flickering flames, and felt better. Now... We had followed the ceremonial "here I intend to camp" to the local spirits before we departed, but it could do no harm to try to reaffirm our presence. Yes, another pinch of tobacco, maybe.

The blue smoke whirled upward into the darkness with my heartfelt prayer. I felt better, but not much. I was having a difficult time with my friend and advisor in this condition. Maybe... What would he have done if he had not been struck with this backward twist?

I decided that he would be here, at the fire, devising some sort of plan. Now, it would fall to me.

"Here. We must eat," I said, handing him another strip of the dried meat.

He took it, but sat holding it in his hand, staring blankly into the darkness.

That was a long night, my friends. I slept little, and Fox stirred restlessly and mumbled from time to time. A time or two I dozed off, into a half-dream world in which time whirled backward and forward again, like the twisting thong of the bow drill. Then I would partially waken and try to distinguish reality from whatever else was happening.

. I thought of going for another look at the river, to see if it had reversed again. This was foreign to anything I had ever heard of. Had the river flowed in the same direction since Creation? Had it only now reversed, and would it run backward for all of that time, back to Creation, before changing again? It was worrisome to me that I could not remember any story, ever, that could fit this pattern. Water simply does not run uphill, does it?

Morning came at last, and I tried to convince myself that Fox appeared a little more alert. That was not easy, yet his eyes seemed to attempt to look, part of the time. I built up the fire, and tried to talk to him. Mostly, I was answered with unresponsive grunts.

I rummaged through a little pack that he had carried, not really knowing what I might be looking for. Among the items in it were small things that a trader might carry... An awl, a small knife, a spoon, a fire striker and flint. There was also a tin cup, such as many whites carry. They use it for many things, as do some of our people now. It is good for dipping from a spring, for heating a little water for tea or the white man's coffee. I found a pouch of pemmican, and an idea came to me. I could heat some of that with water and maybe induce him to eat.

Water, dried and pounded meat, mixed with dried and pounded berries and suet... Yes, maybe.

I quickly prepared the mixture, and impatiently waited for the cup to warm. Its smell was good, as I stirred it over the little fire.

"Here, Fox," I said to him as I approached with a spoonful of the stew. "Open your mouth."

He looked at me blankly, but he did open. I poked the spoon into his mouth and he closed it, sat for a moment and then began to chew. I had to remind him sometimes, but with a lot of patient effort, I managed to get most of the cup into him. I was chewing jerky as I worked.

When the cup was nearly empty, Fox suddenly looked up at me with the first glimmer of understanding I had seen. My heart leaped. Now, maybe we could begin some sort of a plan.

"Fox!" I said. "I am happy that you are awake, Uncle. My heart is good, but we need to plan."

He studied me for a little while, and then spoke slowly.

"Badger, isn't it? What are you doing here? Where are the others?"

"Uncle," I pleaded, "we are looking for White Plume."

"No," Fox protested," White Plume is not here. She is with her mother, helping with the baby."

My heart sank. The trader had tried to go back in time to a better day, maybe, away from the danger. He had seemed to forget the missing girl, in his worry over the backward flow of the river.

Then, another thought struck me. Had Fox's shock over the reversal of flow, and the possible rewinding of time, been a good guess? Was Fox going back with it?

No, no, I thought. I must be going mad. If time has backed up for Fox, why not for me, too? And, he did seem to know me, so not too far back... *Aiee!* It made my head hurt.

Just then, Fox drew his robe around him and lay down near the fire.

"Let's get some rest before we go on," he said. In a moment he was asleep.

I did not know whether that was good or bad. I watched him for a little while, ate some pemmican, and tried to think. Fox's breathing seemed easy, and he seemed to be somewhat better, so I began to plan. I must do something, even if it proved wrong.

Maybe, while he slept, I could complete the circuit around the other side of the town, searching for any trace of White Plume.

CHAPTER NINETEEN

That circuit of the town and the stretch of river along its edge was more puzzling than anything else I might tell you about it. Not only confusing to me, but to those who lived there. There was one man standing, not talking, just staring at the backward flow, his eyes telling that he was dazed. It was as if his spirit had left his body, to try to search for an answer of some sort... any sort, to ease the threat that hovered over us all, that day.

I thought of Fox, back at our camp. I felt, somehow, that the trader had already begun to come back from that in-between world of mystery where he had been the night before. Even so, I must be certain that such a feeling was not simply my wish that it be so.

There were, of course, people who were behaving differently. I saw one house, damaged from the quakes, where people were removing things. Armfuls of clothing, cooking pots and pans, tools... I wondered about it. The house was not badly damaged, and it seemed to me that it could have been repaired. If, of course, one could live in such a place. To me, it would be like a cage or a trap. But Growers do it, and whites... *Aiee*, who knows how they think?

Then it finally occurred to me that maybe the people who had lived there had been killed in the quakes. Or maybe they had moved in with relatives until the weather permitted rebuilding the house.

Or... I watched a little longer. Those who were carrying things out seemed to be in a hurry. They were moving quickly, handing armfuls of clothing, furs, and small things to others on the outside, who hurried away. There were maybe six or eight people involved. It came to me as a surprise. These people were hurrying, glancing around suspiciously as they worked. If they had been helping salvage the possessions of relatives or neighbors, would they not be asking things like "Where shall we put this?" and such. There would be no need to hurry. I had to come to this conclusion: I was watching the stealing of a family's belongings.

At about that time, one of the men yelled at me. I could not tell what he said. I may not have mentioned that these were white men. Of course, I knew almost nothing of their strange tongues, but I could tell that this was not a friendly shout.

I had been warned that when whites are around, it is not good to leave things unguarded. Some whites, of course, are as honest as the People, but it is best to take no chances. About that time, I finally realized that I might be in danger, just from seeing the stealing of someone else's things. I turned and ran.

I saw one other thing on that circuit, which was remarkable to me, as a man of the open prairie. With the land rising and falling, as I told before, there were places that had been under water, now muddy places with dead fishes of all sizes.

Here, near the Big River, which was now running backward, I came upon a sight that struck fear through me. It was a fish, as long as a man is tall. It had a fearsome-looking face, whiskered like that of a cat, with a wide mouth and small beady eyes. The size of that mouth was such that I was made to think: A fish like this could swallow a child easily. Maybe even, a grown man. It had been there for some time, and scavengers had partially stripped the flesh. I decided that I would never swim in any of the waters in that place. Of course, it was winter then, and I would not have done so anyway.

This was only an example of what we were facing. I finished my circle of the town without seeing any trace of the missing White Plume, and my heart was heavy.

I returned to our camp, to find Fox sleeping. That was good, I thought, because he had not rested well for some time. I kept hoping against hope that when he wakened, his spirit might have returned. I had no idea what to do next, and maybe Fox would be able to give us some direction, somewhere to start.

When he awoke, that was only partially true. He was, for sure, not his old self, the calm and confident trader I had come to know and respect.

"I'll get some water," I told him.

We had tried to camp near a spring. There was plenty of water, flooding many places, but usable water was another concern. That whole area is respected for some of the springs that pour healing waters out of the rocks. Even the whites know of this medicine. At that time, though, it had been found that in places where the flooding took place, the water was sometimes poisoned. When we think of it, with the flow of waters backward, of course it would be dangerous. It would be much like drinking downstream from where the buffalo gather, fouling the water. And in this situation, with the Big River running backward, how could we tell? Which is downstream?

Everyone was having the same problem, of course. Plainly, the thing to do was to find a spring where it came out of the rock as far above the ground as possible. Everyone had the same thoughts, and we had tried to select a place for our camp which was near such a spring, but not too near. We had wanted our presence not to be so public as to call attention to it.

I moved slowly, toward the clearing next to the rocky hillside. A white woman was just filling an iron pot, and I slowed my pace a little more, so as not to frighten her.

She finished her task, and looked my way for a moment. She did not seem alarmed, for which I was glad. It is hard to guess how whites will react, especially white women. But we nodded a greeting, both very clumsy about it, and moved on.

I carefully tasted the water, before starting to fill our waterskins. It would be foolish to gulp, when its safety might be in question, no? But the water was good, except for salty tastes that were to be expected. Those healing waters usually smell bad compared to our prairie springs, but it is a different smell than water that is polluted.

From the corner of my eye, I saw someone approaching, and paused to be sure whether there was danger. In such times, there is reason to be suspicious, at least at first. The sight of people robbing the damaged house was still in my mind.

The man paused, as if to avoid any conflict, and I had the chance to look him over a little bit. I had a strange feeling about this man, as if I had known him before. A thing of the spirit, maybe.

At that moment, I could not tell very much about him. He was wearing a buckskin shirt, of a pattern much like our own. This is becoming a common way to dress among some of the whites, especially the trappers and fur traders. Some wear the breech cloth and leggings as we do, others a one-piece garment with the leggings sewn together, and the seat not removable. "Pants," I have heard them called. This man was wearing such a garment. Sometimes these are made of buckskin, but this man's pants were of canvas. Why that impressed me, I do not know.

Maybe it was that I was trying to decide whether it was a white man. He wore moccasins, of the hard-sole plains pattern, which again told little. His hair was long and braided, hanging over his shoulders. The braids were dark, and his face, too, had the look of a skin darker than most whites. And, I saw that he had no face-hair. Of course, some whites pluck their face-hair as the People do, and others scrape it off with the strange knife for cutting face-hair.

I was trying to decide whether this was a fur trapper, a white settler of the town, or maybe even one of the black white men we see sometimes. But, aside from all of those possibilities, there was something that I felt, rather than saw. It was the spirit-thing I mentioned before, maybe, the feeling that we sometimes notice around a holy man of the People. His eyes were fixed on me, watching my every move, yet I felt no danger or threat.

He was tall and thin, and carried himself well, with a quiet confidence. There was something about him that made me think that we had met before. I felt certain that he was no threat. Maybe, even, that this meeting was meant to be.

He raised his empty right hand, palm forward, in the sign understood by nearly everyone: Greetings I bear no weapon. I come in peace.

CHAPTER TWENTY

I was surprised at the formal greeting, and returned the sign.

How are you called? he signed.

It was as if he had been looking for someone.

Badger, I answered.

The man nodded.

Kiowa?

No. Elk-dog People.

"Ah," he spoke aloud, nodding.

"You know my people?" I spoke, but he shook his head, and gave the hand sign for question.

Then began the usual search for a tongue that would be known to both of us, but all in hand signs.

Osage?

No. ... Cheyenne?

No ... Kenza?

Pawnee?

Comanche?

Arapaho?

I finally recalled that Fox often fell back on the languages of some of the eastern tribes who were moving west. I knew a little bit of Cherokee, as I have said before.

With a mix of hand signs, a few words of the white men's Yenglees, and my limited Cherokee, we slowly began to understand each other.

It is hard to explain, but I was made to think that there was some purpose for our chance meeting. The stranger seemed to feel the same.

I do not mean to say that I instantly trusted him. That, of course, would be foolish. As young and inexperienced as I was, I knew enough not to trust strangers. Yet maybe we both felt that we were to work together. There were things about Heron... that was his name, well-called for his tall, thin build. It was easy to see that his name matched his appearance.

This man's whole being gave me the feeling that we sometimes experience around our holy men or women. It is nothing we see or hear or smell or taste, but we are aware of certain things of the spirit. I am made to think that whites do not feel these things as we do. They seem eager to deny any such feelings, as if they are afraid of them. Maybe whites once had this sense of the spirit world and then lost it. Maybe they never had it. But, a white man will argue that a tree, a rock, or a place cannot have a spirit. Yet, they talk of a pleasant place, a happy place, or one filled with gloom. Even their holy men seem not to want to learn about the "Great Mystery," as some call our contact with the spirit world. They say that to try to learn is wrong, and that they can tell us all we need to know. This seems strange, coming from men who honor God only on every seventh day instead of every morning, as the People do.

Yes, forgive me. I was only trying to explain how my meeting with Heron came about. I thought that he must be a holy man, because I felt that he knew things about me that he could have had no way of knowing.

I asked him if he was a holy man.

"No," he protested, "I do a little medicine, that's all."

I learned later that among many people, the custom is to deny any such special gifts, in exactly that way. But, no matter, now.

Heron was of middle age, maybe. It is odd, as I think about it, that I can remember very little about his appearance, except for his resemblance to his namesake bird. I seem to recall graying or whitish hair over his ears, but... *Aiee*, I don't know.

"You are searching for someone?" he asked.

It was not really a question, but a statement. One which I could not deny, of course.

"Maybe," I admitted.

"A woman... "

My temper flared. Did this man have something to do with White Plume's disappearance?

"Do you know..." I almost yelled at him, but he interrupted, using a mix of talk and hand signs.

"No, no, I am trying to help you, Badger, if you will let me. I can see that you are sad, and that you search. It is not hard to guess that the quakes have separated you from someone important to you. For one of your age, most likely a woman, no?"

I had to admit that his thoughts made sense.

"Okeh," I agreed. "Her name is White Plume. She is the daughter of a trader. I work for him."

The man nodded.

"Fox?" he asked.

Again, I was startled. How did this man know so much?

Before I could think to answer, Heron spoke again. "I heard that there was a trader in the area west of here."

"Yes. That is the one. I was traveling with them."

"You do not still do this?"

"Well... yes..."

At this point, I felt that I wanted to blurt out the whole story, yet I knew that it should not be that way.

"You are searching..." Heron suggested.

He had mentioned this before.

"Yes," I admitted.

It was true, I was beginning to see. I was searching for the woman of my lifetime, now missing. But I had already been searching. I had confused my longing for White Plume with my search for the meaning of the world and all that is in it. I had tried to tell my parents that this was a vision quest, which they had not believed, of course. But now I began to see. Maybe it was a vision quest. Where does one mystery stop and another begin? Maybe it is all one Great Mystery, with many parts.

I could probably never have thought of this without the help of Heron, the man I had just met.

Yet, what had he said or done to make me see? Nothing, really. I still knew nothing about him. We had exchanged only a few words. Mostly, except for our first exchange to introduce ourselves, he had asked simple questions. How had it happened that I now felt that this strange man knew everything about me? His questions had not been unreasonable for one I had just met. They had not been prying questions. I had not told him very much.

How had it come to be, then, that I now felt that Heron understood me to the depths of my being? Even more puzzling, the thought that his simple questions and comments had made me understand myself better than I ever had?

Over all of this was the strong feeling that we sometimes feel in the presence of a holy man. It cannot be described, maybe. Things of the spirit are not to be understood, only accepted and treasured.

But...

"I do not understand what is happening here," I blurted finally.

"Badger," Heron said in a kindly way. "If you still think you must understand, you are missing the idea. You must learn to accept."

I had no idea what he was talking about, but I was ready.

I nodded impatiently.

"So... What must I do?"

You see, I was grasping for straws, ready to do whatever I could to find my missing White Plume. But I also wanted to know more about Heron. I did not entirely trust him, but I wanted to. Maybe I could learn more about him.

"You have a woman?" I asked.

His rugged face relaxed for a moment, and he smiled.

"Of course. You met her, no?"

"I think not."

"Oh, yes. At the spring."

I now recalled the woman I had seen, and this brought about more questions than answers, tumbling around in my head. Had the woman mentioned that she had seen me? Had she then told her husband about the encounter? This brought on the more pressing question. If she had done so, in enough detail that Heron recognized me as the one she had seen, why?

Had he then come in search of such a young man? And again, why?

There were surely things going on here that made no sense at all.

CHAPTER TWENTY-ONE

Now, you must remember, it seemed this was happening during the Moon of Madness. Madness had continued through the Moon of Long Nights. The rumbling and shaking of the earth kept on, nearly every day. We were very fortunate that it was not a hard winter... Ah, yes, you laugh, but you know what I mean. There was not very much snow. We were farther south, as well as farther east. Our Southern Band moves south each year, out of the prairie a little way, into the red dirt country, to take advantage of the trees there. The scrubby oaks hold their dead leaves most of the winter. They provide some shelter from Cold Maker's winds.

It was somewhat that way where we were. Farther south, more trees. It was bad enough, but we had no really deep snow, and were not badly exposed to the strong winds of the prairie. I had no way to know what a normal winter might be, in such a place, or when one moon might be shifting into the next. But, as I look back, this must have been sometime in the Moon of Snows. January, the whites call it. It would be a while yet before our Moon of Awakening.

But let me go on... I was trying to explain that so many things were happening which seemed to make no sense at all.

The man, Heron. I had talked to him, and had felt that he was a holy man, and very important to my life and possibly, to White Plume's, if she was still alive. I dared not think otherwise.

Now, out of his presence, I could hardly recall what he looked like. Like a heron, I had thought, but that had been because of his long legs and his body build. His face? I wondered if I would even recognize him the next time we met. A strange thought, no? I knew that I would see him, but questioned if I would know him when I did. In this way, as I look back, I must have been seeing already that here was more of the spirit than is found in most of us. And, his denial of anything special: "I do a little medicine..." should have helped me realize his power as a holy man.

I filled the waterskins and returned to our campfire. Fox was awake, and though he seemed dazed and not quite his usual self, he was somewhat more normal. At least, I felt so.

"Did you find anything?" he asked.

"No. I only went for water," I explained, holding up the waterskins.

For some reason, I did not want to tell him about the meeting with Heron. There was too much of the spirit in that encounter. And, after all, what could I tell him? "I met a strange old man... Well, not old. I don't remember much about him, or what he looked like, but there was something about him."

You can see my problem. I was even arguing with myself about it, and forgetting much of the detail about my chance meeting. Sometimes I wondered if maybe I was being affected by the madness all around me. I had been concerned about Fox, but there were moments when I felt that I, too, might be slipping over the edge of reality into whatever was affecting him. This was not a comfortable feeling, as you might imagine. And, over all of this hung the black cloud of concern for White Plume.

"So, you found good water?" Fox asked.

"Yes. Out of the rock," I answered.

"It is good. But, you learned nothing more?"

"That is true."

I might have told him about Heron, I suppose. But Fox was already moving on. It did not seem to make sense somehow, to bother him with the tale of such an encounter. After all, what could I tell him?

Fox glanced at the sun's position.

"There is daylight left. We could circle the town again. You saw no whites, then?"

"Well, yes, there were several. Some seemed to be looting a damaged house."

"Ah! Did they look like those we seek?

"I don't know, Uncle. I'm not sure that I had ever seen those two. It is hard to look for someone when I don't know what they look like. All whites look alike anyway!"

I had no sooner spoken than I regretted my tone of voice, my attitude, and my disrespect for my elder.

But Fox smiled, more like his old self. Not a happy smile, of course, but one of understanding. "That is true, Badger. But we have to start somewhere. Did you feed the horses?"

No, I had not, and I was ashamed that I had not thought to do it.

"No, I went for water."

It was a lame excuse, and Fox knew it. But he also knew that I knew, and that he need say no more about it. Such was Fox's wisdom

. "It is good," said the trader, though it wasn't, entirely. "Let us chop browse for the horses, and plan from there."

I agreed. It would give me some time to think. I had not decided whether to tell Fox about my encounter with the strange man who called himself Heron, and who knew about our quest.

Fox and I led the horses to an area along a small stream which had a thick growth of cottonwood saplings and began to chop. The horses chewed eagerly, and when we had enough small branches to furnish the day's need, we began to gather wood for our campfire, while the animals finished. I was pleased to see the change in Fox. I had begun to feel a certain desperation, not quite realizing how much it had bothered me.

We returned to our camp, the sun considerably lower now. I was beginning to feel more frustration. Another day, and no progress. What suffering might White Plume be experiencing? My heart was bothered by the same feelings, and that did not help.

We had enough jerky and pemmican for another day or two, and then we must hunt, rather than search, for maybe a day or more. Another reason, I thought, to stay away from towns. All the game in the area would have been hunted out. This, of course, would be a factor in our search for White Plume, if we must stop to hunt. We had made little or no progress so far, and my impatience must have been a burden to Fox. He was probably wondering why they had bothered to save me from the encounter with the buck deer.

It was after dark that I mentioned my encounter with Heron. Instantly, Fox was alert, more like his own keen self. But he was suspicious.

"He knew that you search for a woman?"

"No, no, not like that, Fox. He seemed to know that I search. Like a need for a vision quest, maybe. It was after that, that he reasoned that there must be a woman involved."

Fox was still suspicious.

"Badger, this makes no sense. He asked nothing of you?"

"Nothing! Uncle, you know the feeling that surrounds a holy man? The kind of thing that we cannot see or hear, but we feel the power of his spirit. It was like that. I asked if he was a holy man, but he denied it."

Fox nodded thoughtfully.

"As he should, if he really is," he mused thoughtfully. "But, Badger, there are good medicine men, yet sometimes evil ones."

I had not thought of that.

"But, Uncle, he did not ask anything of me. And he had reasoned that a young man of my age who is troubled is probably troubled over a woman."

"Ah, yes, but it was also this man who brought it into your talk. There is something wrong here. Why should he bother to ask about such a thing?"

"I was made to think he wants to help! He was not trying to learn anything from me, Uncle, but... Look, if he is involved in White Plume's disappearance, he would not want to talk to me. He would avoid us, no?"

Fox was quiet a long time. Finally, he spoke, calmly and quietly.

"Badger, you may be right. He did not say he wants to see you again?"

"No. He did say our trails will cross, or something of the sort."

"Aha!"

"Not like that, Uncle. Look, he mentioned his own wife."

"His wife?"

"Yes. Heron said that I had met her." I had nearly forgotten that.

"And had you?" asked Fox.

"I don't know. There was a woman at the spring. She was there first, and I held back, because she might have been alarmed. You know how white women are, sometimes. She nodded as we passed."

"His wife is a white woman?"

"I don't know! It may not have been the same woman, even."

Fox was puzzled now, and seemed to be pondering.

"I don't know, Badger. This whole thing about the man makes no sense. But, he said you will meet again, no?"

"That is true."

"Ah! Then we will probably learn more when it happens. For now, let us get some sleep, and we will see what tomorrow brings. I look forward to seeing your 'Heron'!"

CHAPTER TWENTY-TWO

It was good to have Fox back, more like himself. Now we could try to plan. But we still had almost nothing to go by. To face this honestly, we were not even certain that the men who had taken White Plume had come this way. They might have turned off on any of the narrow trails that crisscross that area.

But to think in such a way was not good. I would rather think of the mysterious man I had met. In a way I could not explain, I felt better when I thought of Heron. And it seemed, in my mind anyway, that he had promised help. I had no idea how, or when or where.

We built up the fire so that we would not have to start a new one. Enough to keep it going, the spark of life that we could blow into flame when we would return. While we chewed some strips of dried meat, we talked about how to continue our search.

I suggested that we make another circle around the town, trying to notice anything that did not seem to be normal. Of course, there had been nothing that seemed normal since the Moon of Madness, anyway. How would we be able to tell?

It was a crisp, cool morning, a gray, overcast sky. Small wisps of fog hung motionless among the trees and bushes. We would stay together on this circuit. I thought that maybe Fox wanted to keep an eye on me. Not that he distrusted me, but I have to admit that my tale of the mysterious "Heron" must seem questionable at best. I almost doubted it myself.

We both carried bows and a couple of arrows. There might be an opportunity to try for some fresh meat if we encountered a rabbit or squirrel. It was not likely, since we wanted to be near where there were people. But it would be foolish not to be armed, no? I had a knife in the thong at my waist, and Fox, a small axe, the kind whites call a "tomahawk." It was handy for cutting cottonwood browse for the horses, but could also be a weapon if needed. Fox was skilled with it, and could throw it at a target with much force and accuracy. He did not demonstrate this skill very often, but I had once seen him showing Toad the proper way to throw the weapon. I might have learned something if I had watched and listened. But, I didn't. I was so irritated by Toad's teasing, and his interference with my ambitions for romance with White Plume... *Aiee* , the things I might have done differently! At that time, I had been a childish disaster waiting to happen. Now, at least, I was aware that there was much that I did not know.

The urgency of the situation brought me back to reality.

"Let us head north," Fox decided, "then turn east, on around and back to here."

I did not question, but it came to me that to circle in this manner would be the same direction as the ceremonial pipe is handed in a formal council circle of any kind. Each member of the circle, facing toward the center, passes it to the one on his left. It could do no harm, to follow such a formality. Possibly, no help either, but it did lend a bit of confidence.

I had never seen Fox walk so slowly. His eyes were never still, glancing from side to side, pausing to observe any new thing he may chance to notice. Yet, he managed to keep an appearance of unconcern, as if this was only a pleasant stroll.

We saw several small camps like our own. We were watched with what seemed to me to be suspicious looks, especially from some of the whites. But, that was nothing new. I was learning to ignore it.

We were nearing the place where I had found the water, a spring in the rocky hillside. I was about to explain this to Fox, but a small motion caught the corner of my eye. I turned and watched as a large bird soared in for a landing beyond a grove of trees. I could not see it well, I admit. I was looking through the bare winter limbs. The bird disappeared behind some scrubby cedars, but it seemed that it must have landed. I thought it was strange for a bird the size of an eagle or a large hawk to be landing so near to where so many people were moving around. Still, I did not really think of this as unusual, especially in a time when everything else had been so strange.

I turned slightly to look, and saw, near a muddy little pool, a tall bird, the blue heron so commonly seen in wet places. Yes, I see your doubts. This is a summer bird, which winters far to the south, and returns in the Moon of Greening. This was not yet even the moon before. The herons should not be returning for another moon or two.

Maybe, I thought, herons could winter here, but that made no sense. We were still too far north. I glanced at Fox, and it appeared that he did not see the bird at all, or was looking somewhere else. I looked back... Ah! My eyes had deceived me.

What I had seen as a long-legged bird was in fact, a man, the one I knew as "Heron." The wisp of fog had helped the deception. I was also seeing him at a greater distance, appearing smaller than he actually was. Besides all this, he had been holding, and partly leaning on, a short lance or spear. He wore a cape against the foggy morning, and it hung down around his shoulders to about his waist. I cannot describe it any better, but the combination of long, straight legs, the spear shaft, and the shape of the hanging cape resembling folded wings...

For a moment I almost believed that I had seen the heron change into a man. Yes, I understand that you will laugh at this. But you were not there.

It is hard to explain how I could have made such a mistake, but... Well, he had been standing on one leg, the other foot drawn up with his foot propped against his knee. This gave an appearance much like that of his namesake bird, who often stands on one leg, the other drawn up for the next cautious step. There are still times when... But never mind, I will go on.

"This is the man I told you of," I told Fox as we approached. He nodded, without answering.

Heron held up his right palm in the gesture of greeting, and Fox returned it, as I did also.

The man was much as I remembered, lanky and tall, with long legs and arms, dressed in a buckskin shirt and trousers. His hair was long and braided, and he wore a fur hat. Again, I was not certain... He might be a white man. His face was clean, without hair. His eyes, I could not tell. They were dark, but of course, some whites do have brown eyes, you know.

There was a short time while the two men tried to find a language with which to talk. It was easier than it had been for me, since Fox knew many tongues. They soon arrived at a mix which would be usable. Most of it, I understood, and where I did not, they were helpful to me.

"Badger has said that you may be a help to us," Fox said.

"Maybe..."

"You have seen her?"

"The girl? Maybe..."

This began a strange conversation. It was plain to see that Heron did know or had seen, something important. I also had the feeling that for some reason, he was unable to share all that he knew with us. That was frustrating, of course, but still, I had the strong feeling that Heron was helping us as much as he could. It was as if to tell us too much might cause his medicine not to work.

"Tell me more about the girl," he spoke to Fox. "She is your daughter, no?"

"That is true."

"It is good," nodded Heron thoughtfully.

I did not see any reason that he should be making such a statement. I saw almost nothing that I could clearly call good.

"We will try some medicine," said Heron. "Come."

We followed him a short distance along a winding path in the woods, and we approached a lodge made of logs, as the whites often use. I thought again, how odd it was that I was trusting this stranger. But, Fox was doing the same. There was a moment of panic as I wondered how we could have been so stupid as to trust a stranger we had never seen, to expect him to help us.

About then, a woman came out of the lodge, and came toward us, smiling a welcome. It was the woman I had seen at the spring.

"My wife," explained Heron. "She saw young Badger, when he came to the spring, and told me of your need for help."

"She is a seer?" asked Fox.

"She does a little medicine," said Heron, "as I do. Sees Beyond, she is called."

I needed to know more about this strange couple. They were a complete mystery. Or maybe two separate mysteries. I had never met anyone about whom I knew less than I did about these two. The woman's name told much: Sees Beyond. But, we still did not know any more about her. About either of them, really.

But I recalled her reaction when we met at the spring. I had thought that she, a white woman, was alarmed at seeing me.

Now, it appeared that her alarm may have been not over me, but over my problem. Her gift of concern must be very powerful. She must have gone home, told Heron about her feelings, and he had come to meet me and see for himself the weight of my troubles.

Now I was completely confused. I was not certain whether Sees Beyond was a white woman, even. Or, about Heron, either. Here, I began to realize, was a powerful team of seers. How and why we had come together, I did not know. I was still somewhat suspicious but I kept reminding myself: If one with the gift of the spirit uses it for anything but good, he not only loses the gift, but he may be destroyed by its power. I had that to hold to. I only hoped that this was true, not only among the People, but among whatever tribe or tribes might be represented in this couple's lodge.

The lodge itself meant nothing. As I said, it was of logs, much like those of the whites. But, many of the tribes moving from the east had already lived in towns, like the whites. Or, like some of the Growers, in the country of our People.

Their clothing gave little information, either. I have mentioned that Heron wore buckskins, but many white trappers do. His cape, too, was more like a short blanket, for warmth at this time of year. It was of fur.

Looking at Sees Beyond now, I wondered why I had even thought she was a white woman at all. In her own lodge, where she was now, she stood calm and confident.

I began to realize some things I did not yet understand, then. In some of these eastern tribes, the woman owns all the property. Her husband was nearby, but she was confident for herself. The expression of doubt on her face when she saw me had not been from fear. Her concern was for me, and the troubles that I had been facing. Heron explained this to me, later. Sees Beyond had felt the weight of my problems, and had told Heron when she arrived back at their lodge. This had caused him to come and look for me.

Why, I do not pretend to understand. We do not question why men or women with gifts of the spirit do the things they do.

CHAPTER TWENTY-THREE

I learned later, Sees Beyond had a very strange childhood. She was white, as I have said. Some of Heron's people had found her as an infant, only a few moons old, it seems. Her parents were dead at their camp, from some sickness. The mother had been dead for a day or two. Her body was in their wagon, wrapped in a blanket. The man had tried to care for the baby, but he must have been dying, himself. Their horses were loose, browsing near the camp. The man sat on the ground with his back against a tree, holding the baby in his lap. It was screaming. He had not been dead very long.

Heron's people quickly saw the situation, and the danger that it meant for them. The sickness that had killed the parents must carry a dangerous spirit. There were those who thought that the only thing to do was to leave as quickly as possible. The baby would probably die anyway, and would be a danger if they tried to take care of it.

They might have left it, but a respected holy woman studied the scene and the dead bodies, and decided to take the baby with her.

"I like the way it yells. This is a special child. Its spirit is strong."

Sees Beyond was raised by the medicine woman, and by an early age, was showing her own gift of understanding. Her foster mother named her "Sees Beyond," and treated her as an apprentice. It must have been a strange childhood, growing up in a family where the mother was a seer, but a "brother," who was called Heron, also. He had shown, very early, his own gifts of the spirit.

It seemed strange to me that a white baby would be seen to have gifts of the spirit, no? Sees Beyond helped us to understand. She is a very wise seer. It is her feeling that not only her people and ours, but all of the native peoples have those who are given spirit-gifts. Some refuse them because of the responsibility involved, and that is acceptable. But they then lose the power, of course. We understand this.

Sees Beyond went farther in her explanation, though. We have always felt that whites almost never have the gifts of the spirit. Even the holy men of the whites do not seem to understand. Any but their own, they see as "bad" spirits, and they do not trust. So, they deny many of the spirit-happenings that are clear to our people.

But Sees Beyond and Heron feel that all humans are offered this closeness to the spirit-world. Yenglees, French, Spanish, and even the "black white man." Most refuse it, because they have been taught that it is bad. I had never seen these black white men, but Heron said that they may have a little more of the spirit gifts. Most of the whites, though, have been taught from childhood: If you see anything you do not understand, be afraid of it, because it is not real. So, they miss out on many things of the spirit. They are taught from childhood to refuse the gifts that our people cherish, so having refused, they have lost them. Is sad, no?

But back to the woman, Sees Beyond. She had lost her white parents before she was old enough to be taught anything. So, her special gifts, instead of being lost, as in most whites, were nurtured by her foster mother, who was a powerful seer. She must have been, to raise these two children. Both of them have since proved to have very powerful guides.

I know that I am wandering from my story, but be patient with me. You will see that it is a part of my story.

Sees Beyond had seen me at the spring, and had felt my trouble. She must have felt my pain and frustration, and her heart reached out to me. She had hurried to tell Heron, who then came back to look for me. *Aiee*, their ways are hard to understand, so I was made to think that I must explain a little about this strange couple.

At one point, I was ready to say that I have actually seen Heron change into his namesake bird and fly away. Then, I think again, no, that cannot be. It only looked so. Then, I would remember that there are few herons in winter, and I would think that there must be things of the spirit happening. In my frustration, I finally asked Heron outright:

"What is happening? I do not understand!"

Heron, always wise and usually gentle, smiled. Maybe a little sadly, I thought.

"Badger," he said, "if you still think you have to understand... Did we not speak of this before? Some things are not meant to be understood, only respected."

Of course, I remembered now, and felt foolish. This added to my frustration.

I apologize for neglecting my story to tell you of more about Heron and Sees Beyond. But, they were quickly to become a part of my story.

Sees Beyond asked more questions about White Plume, and about the rest of the family, Fox's wife and whether there were any other children. It was plain that the more she knew about White Plume and her family, the better she could try to reason what had happened, and what must be happening now.

Somehow, her serious, steady manner was reassuring to me, as well as to Fox.

Already, we were growing in our confidence. Now, it seemed, we had help. Until now, we had been slogging around, as if we were wading deep mud.

Well, sometimes we were wading mud, yes. But you know what I mean. We had been aimlessly stumbling along. Now I felt, with the help of this odd pair, that we had some direction, some growing plan.

I was sure that Fox felt it, too. He was regaining some of his old demeanor. It was good to see him becoming himself again.

You may be wondering how and maybe, why we were so quick to accept this help from people we did not even know. Yes, looking back it seems odd, but I cannot explain it. Why should these people put themselves into danger for us, a pair of strangers? Again, I must say, some things are not meant to be understood, only accepted. At the time, it seemed reasonable. It was as if Heron and Sees Beyond saw this as a task they had been given.

"Maybe," the woman said, "it would be easier if you moved your camp over here."

She gestured to a small clearing to the west of their house.

"What about the horses?" asked Fox.

"There is browse," pointed Heron. "You will need to cut it somewhere. Why not here?"

It was good, and seemed reasonable at the time. Probably, we were becoming desperate, and were ready for anything that resembled a plan. We did not question. We moved our camp.

In a way, it was a great relief. I had been worried each time we left our camp unguarded. If one of us was near, it was unlikely that any intruder would even think of trying to steal anything of value. Of course, we had almost nothing of value. This would be apparent to any intruder.

Our weapons, we would be carrying. About the only things worth stealing were our horses. Even so, to steal horses in an area with many people would be risky. Except, of course, for one thing: Many of the people in the area were whites, and some of them are not to be trusted. They actually steal not only from other people, it seems, but from each other! So, you can see that it was an attractive invitation that Sees Beyond offered to us.

We moved that afternoon, and during the time we were gone, it seemed that the holy woman had spent her time with some complicated and mysterious ceremony. Heron mentioned this when we returned.

Sees Beyond was moving around a small fire a little distance from the house, shaking a pair of rattles and singing as she danced.

Heron met us as we approached.

"Sees is doing a ceremony," he explained. "Let us not bother her. This one needs all of her attention. You could set up your camp over there."

He pointed, with a shrug of his shoulder.

"It is good!" answered Fox. "We will do so."

CHAPTER TWENTY-FOUR

Their house itself was very different. I know, I keep repeating myself when I speak of this couple. But, I must try to tell you...

I had, before this, been in the lodge of a holy man only a few times. Or a holy woman, of course. Our own Southern band has a medicine woman, Snakewater. Yes, I will go on.

When we stepped into the log cabin lodge of Heron and Sees Beyond, my first sensation was that of smell.

It was strong, but not overwhelming. Interesting, familiar somehow, and not unpleasant. Of course, I realized, scent is very important to a medicine person. The spirits respond more to smell than to any of human sensations. That is why we burn a pinch of tobacco in any new fire. It tells the spirits "I am here," and asks their tolerance and favor.

I had not thought about this very deeply until now. I had been too involved in childish thoughts and desires and needs to think of much, except my own selfish likes and dislikes.

In the lodge of these medicine-people, as my eyes became adjusted to the dim light, I noticed many bundles of dry herbs and plants of all kinds, hanging from the poles that supported the roof. Some, I could identify, others were strange to me. I began to see that the smells of all these dried bundles add up to a powerful mix. Each is different from the others, used for a special purpose. Each spirit, good or bad, must be related to a scent.

Some of these would probably be used to please a particular spirit, as tobacco pleases the spirits of a place. Others could be used to attract a helpful spirit to fight a bad spirit, healing and restoring health. For any sickness, I now began to understand, the medicine-person must know which plant will please or displease the spirits involved. *Aiee*, what a task!

All of the scents of these drying plants and roots and berries mingled together into a rich mix, not unpleasant, but powerful. I nearly said, a "soup." That was the way it struck me. A soup may be made of many flavors mixed together. Meats, sometimes more than one, potatoes, beans, onions, pumpkins... on and on. We do not taste a single flavor, but the blend. I am made to think that the scents in this lodge of the holy people had the same sort of blend in it, but a blend of scent, not taste.

The furnishings in the house were simple, but looked comfortable. A bed, on the floor, at the opposite end from the fireplace, which was built in the white man's style. We did notice that Sees Beyond did most of her cooking outside when weather permitted. Most do that in any tribe, I suppose. Maybe even whites, I don't know.

But now began the task, for Sees Beyond, of trying to learn all she could of White Plume. She would try to find a way to see what she could about White Plume's welfare, as well as her location.

"Do you have anything she might have touched?" Sees Beyond asked.

Fox and I looked at each other, somewhat blankly, I must admit. What sort of a thing, and why? Then I saw what she meant. An object handled by the missing White Plume might hold traces of her thoughts; of her spirit. Sees Beyond might be able, with her special spirit-gifts, to mingle this with some of her own answers to the problem which faced us.

As these thoughts raced through my head, my hand reached toward my chest. I had not thought of it until now, in terms of help for our seemingly helpless situation. Swinging on a thong beneath my buckskin shirt was an oddly-shaped stone, which no one knew about except two persons: Myself and White Plume.

We had been camped, before even the first of the earthquakes, in a pleasant place... Yes, I have told you of that.

We had camped on a beautiful creek, with a white gravel streambed. You know the kind. Clean water, clear as a summer sky, whispering and chuckling over the stones. It has done so since Creation, maybe, smoothing and polishing down the sharp edges. There is always a variety of shapes, much like the shapes we see in clouds in summer. They might look like a bird, an animal, or a flower, or maybe just a round ball, carved by time and the constant rolling and polishing of the stream.

White Plume had found one of these stones which was flat and thin, rounded on all edges, and with a small hole near one edge. It was a small pretty thing, maybe two fingers across.

If I had found it, I might have given it to her. We both looked at it, handled it, and talked of its warm feel, even on a cold day, and taken from cold water.

"Its spirit is good," said White Plume. "I give it to you."

Before I realized what she was doing, she had cut a thong or two from the fringe on her dress and knotted them together, threading it through the hole in the pretty stone. She looped it over my head like a pendant.

"There," she said. "It will remind you of me when you feel it against your heart."

I was embarrassed, of course. I had no gift to give in return. Besides, I did not know how her parents might react. I thanked her, and tucked the pendant inside my shirt.

It was not long after that, when White Plume disappeared. And yes, Fox had never heard of this until now. At least, he did not show anger.

Sees Beyond almost became excited over this. I handed her the stone, still on its thong, and she cradled it between her palms, closed her eyes, and tilted her head back. For a moment, I almost thought that I could see her spirit as it reached out, searching.

Then she took a deep breath, opened her eyes, and smiled. It was the first time that I had seen that expression. Not that her face was overly serious or sad at other times, but this was almost a feeling of excitement.

"This is exactly what we need!" Sees told me. "This is a thing of great importance to the two of you, no?"

I nodded, embarrassed, but excited that Sees Beyond could tell from this simple stone... Well, she was aptly named!

"This will take a little time," the holy woman assured us. "There is a ceremony; private, you see. For now, I am made to feel that the one whose spirit clings to this stone is alive. I will try to visit her, and learn more."

"Will White Plume know your spirit is searching for her?" asked Fox.

"I don't know. Maybe. We will have to see what happens. Heron will bring you news."

We left their lodge and went back to our new campsite. The horses seemed content, and daylight was fading. We could chop browse for them in the morning.

Neither of us could think of sleeping. We kept the fire going, but we talked little. Our thoughts were probably similar, almost afraid to be too hopeful, yet more so than we had been for some time. A little while after dark, Heron came out of the house and joined us. He squatted across the fire from where the two of us sat, under our makeshift lean-to. Fox invited him to come around to the warmer side, but Heron brushed the suggestion away with a wave of his hand.

"I won't stay. Sees has started her ceremony."

"May we know how long it will take?" asked Fox. Heron smiled.

"I don't know. Sometimes she doesn't know, maybe. But she wanted me to tell you, after she got started. Now, for a while, I cannot know what is happening. She leaves our lodge, in spirit, to go to some other level. Sometimes I get a hint, a thought or two. That is why I came over. I was made to think that Sees has made a contact of some sort."

"Then, White Plume is alive?" blurted Fox.

"It would seem so," Heron said cautiously. "If not, Sees Beyond would have hurried back. Now, I go home to be there when her spirit returns. That might be any time, or much later. I will tell you what I learn."

That was the longest night of my life. At least, up until that time. We knew that it must take time, but we had no way of knowing how much time our White Plume might have, before... I dared not think of some of the things that might be happening to her. Or, what may have happened already. And my heart was pounding with a mixture of hope, fear, and dread. My friends, may you never have to face a night like that one.

CHAPTER TWENTY-FIVE

Daylight finally showed in the east. A clear day, it appeared. There was a light tremor just as the eastern sky began to pale, but we were accustomed to such things now. We did not even speak of it as we rose and stirred up the fire.

We both kept glancing anxiously at the house, and were rewarded, finally, by a wisp of white smoke from the chimney. We waited, what seemed a long time. It was fully light, but the sun had not yet risen, when the door opened and Heron made his way toward us. It was very good to see a smile on his usually stern face.

"Sees is back," he called ahead. "It is good."

My heart soared like the eagle.

"Come," he said, smiling. "Let us eat and Sees will tell us where she has been. It is good, she says."

It had been a long time since I had been able to see anything good about anything. I jumped to my feet.

"What... where...?" I mumbled, but Heron waved me aside.

"I don't know, Badger. Sees Beyond will tell us, but she seems pleased by what she knows. Come!"

Fox was rolling out of his blankets and scrambling to his feet.

"Go ahead and empty bladders if you need to," Heron offered. "Then come to the house."

Sees Beyond is not a person who smiles easily. I have always thought that a holy man or woman cannot be expected to laugh very much or to appear to be very happy. The weight of responsibility that falls on the shoulders of a seer must be heavy. Because of this, many who are offered the gifts of the spirit do refuse them.

I thought of this as we entered and our eyes became accustomed to the dimness of the house. Sees Beyond was sitting near the fireplace, hands spread to catch the warmth of the fire. It was a frosty morning. The holy woman had, on her face, an odd expression. Not a smile, exactly, but a look of calm satisfaction, while some worry or concern still showed. All in all, though, she seemed to glow with confidence.

This was a great help to me. Instantly, I felt better. It may seem strange, that as bad as the situation was, I would feel better. Looking back, the thought that any of this could possibly turn out well was a very slim chance. But, if there are two chances, slim and none, "slim" begins to look better and better. The main thing, of course, was the attitude of the holy woman, and her calm look of confidence. Surely, she knew of things beyond the understanding of most of us. These things, I do not pretend to understand. But, it is not necessary to understand a thing of the spirit to accept, to honor, to be grateful for it.

All of this occurred to me later, of course. At the time, I was impatient. I surely did not comprehend the things that were going on. But to look at the calmness that Sees Beyond now showed was to trust her.

The holy woman said very little while we ate. This was understandable. She had been under great stress and effort, and must eat to regain her strength. As for ourselves, Heron urged us to eat. I got the feeling, as I chewed the pemmican, that Heron was preparing us for action of some sort. We must have the strength and the energy for whatever was to happen. I did not realize until later that he, too, knew nothing of what Sees Beyond was to tell us. Heron was acting on her attitude, and her reaction to her vision just past.

It seemed a long time before Sees Beyond began to brighten. She had eaten, and had sipped at a tin cup that had been warming at the fireplace. It seemed to be that it took some time, as well as some food and drink, to come back from wherever she had been in the world of the spirits. I had always understood that such a journey is demanding, not only to the mind, but physically. Now, I was seeing it. It was more disturbing to watch than I had expected. *Aiee*, I don't know what I expected.

Finally, Sees Beyond shifted her position a little, took a deep breath, and turned to look directly at Fox. There was a tone of sympathy in her glance, in recognition of the suffering he must be feeling, but her smile was encouraging to me. It was not a look of helpless pity, but something better.

"Your daughter is a proud one, and strong," she began. "That has served her well. And, she is much wiser than those who took her. That has helped, too."

The smile on the face of the holy woman seemed almost to reflect amusement for a moment.

"There are two, as we suspected. Trappers."

"Whites?" asked Fox quickly.

"Maybe. Or, half-breed. They do know some of our native ways. Enough for them to worry about. And the girl is using this."

Sees went on, telling us what she had learned. I still do not understand how, but that was a part of her medicine, not to be understood by most of us.

"You have seen her, talked to her?" Fox asked impatiently.

The withering glance of the holy woman stopped him short.

"Of course not," she said indignantly. "I am trying to tell you."

"Forgive me," mumbled Fox.

"I understand," said Sees Beyond. "I know it must be hard. But let me tell it."

Fox nodded an apology and agreement, and she accepted with a nod.

"Okeh!"

We had noticed that this word, Cherokee for "it is good" was being used by many people, even whites. Even so, it was a surprise to hear it from the medicine woman. But, I will go on.

Sees Beyond told how she had used the stone from around my neck to search for a spirit connection to our White Plume. In this way, she had an invisible contact by which she could learn the girl's mood, the good and not-so-good feel for her spirit. In body, I suppose that Sees never left the house, but in spirit...

"White Plume is not injured. She was treated roughly when she was taken. Tied, and her mouth covered. She was wise enough to appear to be helpless, so that they would become careless. Also, wise enough to turn one against the other. As I have said, these two are not very bright in their heads. They had thought to sell her, and she has convinced them that she is worth more if she is undamaged. True, of course. But, when she is alone with one, she pretends fear of the other, and begs protection. Now, they no longer trust each other."

Heron chuckled. He had apparently not heard any of this before.

"A wise child," he remarked.

"This is true. A special young woman," agreed the seer.

"What do we do now?" demanded Fox. "And, where are they? Near here?"

Sees Beyond hesitated for a moment.

"I cannot tell you," she admitted.

Fox's impatience began to grow.

"Can't, or won't?" he demanded. "This is my daughter!"

Heron intervened quickly.

"Of course, friend. I can understand your pain. We had a daughter. We lost her. But, what Sees is telling you... Well, in the spirit-world there is not the 'here' and 'over there.' Not as we know it in our bodies. The four winds are not the same."

"That is true," agreed Sees Beyond. "A thing that cannot be described. I can tell much about their camp, but its location, maybe we have to find."

I had another thought.

"Mother," I addressed her with respect, "will White Plume know that you were there, in spirit?"

The woman gave me a long look, as if she had not seen me before. It was a critical look, maybe, telling me that I did not understand the situation. Then she softened a little, seeming to feel my concern.

"Badger," she said in a more kindly voice, "I do a little medicine, that's all. In the spirit world, things are different. Maybe there is no 'time' or 'place.' Maybe it is like looking through a grove of trees, at something out on the grassland. As we move along we can see through openings in the woods, a short look at what is beyond. Sometimes we see some things clearly... Buffalo, maybe. A short glimpse, then gone. How many, how far? Who is to know? And when, or how, or even why?

"Now, what will White Plume know of my attempt to look across by the spirit? I cannot tell. White Plume might sense that someone she loves is trying to do something to help her. And that is good. I tried to leave her every sign that I could, and I am made to think that White Plume is wise beyond her years. She will know that something is being done."

There was a long silence, and finally Fox spoke. His tone was one I had never heard before, a sort of apology.

"Mother," he began, using the address of respect, though there was probably little difference in their ages, "my heart is heavy, that I spoke in anger to one who tries to help. I... "

"It is nothing," Sees Beyond shrugged off the apology. "Now, let us begin to plan."

In a camp nearly a half day's travel away, White Plume woke and began to carry out her morning chores. She was puzzled at some of the night-visions that had come to her. She had dreamed of her parents and of a stranger, a medicine woman, who carried a pendant, a stone taken from the gravel of a murmuring stream It took her only a moment to remember that stone as she came fully awake. She had placed it on a thong and over the head of Badger, who must be now thinking of her. This morning, she found herself more optimistic than she had been for days.

CHAPTER TWENTY-SIX

Of course the first thing to do must be to locate the camp of those who had taken White Plume. Sees Beyond felt that it was not far away. Maybe a half-day's walk. But, in what direction? There must be a way to discover them.

Even then, it could be a dangerous situation. Anyone who would steal a young woman might do nearly anything. True, their deeds had marked them as cowards, but also as men without moral character. When trapped, they might fight like a winter bear.

I repeat what we all know: The People have had a covenant with Bear since Creation. We do not hunt Bear, or eat him, and in return, he does not hunt us. Sometimes, of course, there is an accident, a misunderstanding. To stumble onto a winter bear during his time of sleep is to face great danger. Bear, in his sleep-broken anger, forgets the covenant.

Bear has a reason for his behavior. These men, we feared, had no covenant with anyone. They cannot justify what they have done, so they would be expected to fight, or even to kill, without further cause and without warning, anyone who even questions their actions.

We talked of this, and about what approach might be best. Sees Beyond suggested that we separate, and scout the area as if hunting. Two thieves would not see a lone hunter as much of a threat. But, two armed men would draw closer attention. We also agreed that we must make no attempt alone to free White Plume.

Again, I fell to worrying about what treatment White Plume might have had to endure. Sees Beyond had gone to some length, without saying so, to hint that a young woman might be more valuable merchandise in trade if she had not been sexually abused. I wondered if the holy woman was only trying to be kind to me, to help me in my dread. Or maybe, Sees only wanted to remind me that White Plume might have been a victim of repeated rape, or even worse, torture. Our best hope was that her abductors were greedy for her value in trade. The entire situation was not good, but possibly better than before we had the help of Sees and Heron.

We decided, with the approval of Heron, that Fox could act as a hunter, circling the area north of the settlement, as far as the river. I would do the same to the south, except that I would appear to be looking for firewood, with my bow slung across my back. Both would appear not unusual in this place and time. Most of the people we had seen for the past moon were doing these same things. Most, also, appeared dazed and aimless. It is hard to have a goal of any sort when all there is to expect is the unexpected.

For some, this was already leading to madness. Think of it this way: We look at a hill, and decide to climb it, for whatever purpose. Just to see the other side, maybe. But before we start to climb, another quake flattens the hill. Of what use is any plan? And, about the time we decide that the tremors are quieting some, comes another. Maybe it was good that we had something to keep our attention on our goal, to free White Plume. That was more important to me than the movement of mountains or that the Miss-iss-ippi ran backwards.

But forgive me. Back to my story.

I was following a path around the south edge of the village, carrying a few sticks to make my actions more believable, when I saw a young man coming toward me, apparently also gathering fuel. We nodded a greeting, and were about to move on, when another tremor struck.

By this time, my reactions had become a routine. At the beginning, one learns to stand still until the strength of the tremor shows itself. There is no place to run, anyway, and moving rapidly only makes it easier to stumble or lose your footing. I stopped, and so did the other man, waiting to see what would happen next. This might be the first of a cluster of shocks.

Our eyes met as we paused, and the other smiled. That was a welcome thing. I smiled back. Neither of us knew whether or not we were in trouble, but if we were, we both had the same problem. There was a space of several heartbeats, and the other man began to relax.

These are strange times, he said, using hand signs.

That is true, I answered him.

We both laughed nervously.

You live here? he asked.

Somewhat earlier, I would have been at a loss to answer, and would probably have embarrassed myself with a stupid answer, but I was changing somewhat. I needed to be vague about being here.

No, I answered. Just visiting. Hunting a little. There was a long pause as we both waited to feel the half-expected next tremor, but nothing happened. We began to relax a little.

Well, good hunting, signed the other.

I would normally have passed on, but for some reason, I signed to him again.

You live here? I asked.

Yes, he signed. Many new people. We don't understand why.

I had not really thought about it myself, why so many people were moving at this time of year. Normally, everyone would have settled down somewhere for their winter's stay. Like the Bear, almost. But this season of madness had all but destroyed custom and tradition. People of all tribes and nations were still moving around, feeling insecure as a result of solid earth that was no longer solid, but moving and shaking. Everybody felt a need to do something, but had no idea what it should be, or where or when. I am made to think that people can usually handle many troubles, but not the unknown.

I was not thinking of this at the moment, of course. I had simply formed a brief kinship, there on the path, with another of my own age, because we shared the same problem, the quakes.

How are you called? I asked in hand signs.

Red Dog. Usually just Red, he laughed. You?

I am Badger. Badger.

There was a short silence, and then both of us laughed. I cannot explain, maybe, but it struck both of us at once. Why was it that someone called Red Dog in his own tongue was sometimes called "Red?" In my own name, it was only "Badger," but never anything else. This is the sort of thing that does not translate easily, even with the help of hand signs.

Who are your people? I signed.

Red Dog attempted to tell me, but I did not know the tribal names he was using, and we soon gave it up. There were many foreigners in the area, and many displaced and homeless because of the shaking of the earth. Yours? he asked.

Elk-dog People. Buffalo hunters. A long way from home! I answered. I travel with a trader – Arapaho.

I was beginning to be uncomfortable about this. I was giving out far more information than I had intended. Still, it was good to talk with anyone not concerned in my own problems.

I was wanting to hurry on, when Red Dog began to sign again.

These are strange times. Somebody tried to sell a woman to my father.

I tried to resist the temptation to demand the whole story, which was very hard for me.

A woman? I signed. Where? I tried to ask casually.

The other man shrugged.

Who knows? They do not say. Only to interested buyers, maybe. My father was. . .

At that time, our hand-sign talk was working very well. Red Dog used the signs for "sick" and for "sad" and one for "angry." Maybe, though, hand signs were the only way to find words for the disgust that Red Dog and his father felt over the situation.

Now, I was faced with a big decision. Here was a possibility that we could find and help White Plume. But if many people knew about our search, surely word would travel back to those who held the girl. I decided to change the subject, but it was very hard to back off.

Where are you camped? I asked.

Red pointed, with a tilt of his head. That way, maybe two bow shots. You?

That way, a little farther. I indicated the way I had come.

I had been glad to see that when Red Dog pointed, he did not use his hand. Some of the other tribes, and whites, of course, do not seem to understand that any bad spirits in the area can watch a finger-point and go there to cause trouble. We already had all the trouble that we could handle. Maybe more.

CHAPTER TWENTY-SEVEN

This begins a new and dangerous part of our story. I was trying to be very cautious about how much to say to Red Dog or his family. Still, it was hard not to like him. He showed great sympathy for the captive woman. He had not even seen her, only heard whispers and rumors. Still, his heart appeared to be right. His talk, the way he spoke of a woman for sale or trade, showed his upbringing to be much like that of the People.

It seems strange to us that there are some tribes who do not hold the respect for women that we are taught among the People. I am made to think that the worst are probably the whites. I had never seen many of them until this Winter of Madness, but I quickly learned. Their ways are very different, but just as among native peoples, there are good and bad ones. Some treat their women better than others, the same as among us. Still... as you know... I had learned that among whites, most women cannot even speak in Council, or own property, except for their cooking pots, spoons, knives, and such. They cannot even vote, I am told. I am made to think that such treatment would not be tolerated by our women.

It was finally becoming clear to me that White Plume's status was that of a slave, with no rights at all. This was another thing I was beginning to learn. The People have had slaves sometimes, captured in war, though not often in my lifetime. Usually they are traded or sold back to their people or to others. Some have brought themselves up to become respected as members of the People, by proving themselves worthy.

Yes, I know I am rambling, but it is important. I must explain that the status of any woman held by these two whites was very dangerous. They would have no respect for anything except the price that she would bring. That would be more if she had not been disfigured, despoiled, or mutilated in some way. This was our best hope, though it wasn't much. My heart was heavy, and I was about to explode with impatience, like a stone taken from a stream and placed too near the fire. The spirits of water and fire cannot live together. I was starting to think that my own spirit could not survive even the thought of anyone mistreating White Plume.

I began to think on what tortures I would wish to perform on her captors if opportunity offered. Scalping alive was too kind a treatment for such a man. Maybe the removal of a finger at a time, or ears, or some other appendages I might consider, leaving such a poor excuse for a human alive to suffer.

I finally drew myself up short, as one would stop a horse at the end of the race. Had the madness warped my mind? What was I thinking, to have such thoughts pounding in my head? If ever I needed to be steady and thoughtful, it was now. I must keep close contact with Red Dog, but keep him from knowing why.

Maybe we could hunt together? I signed. Show me where your lodge is.

Maybe, answered Red Dog. A canvas teepee, near that big sycamore.

He pointed with a nod of his head again, and that was good.

May I meet you there in the morning?

It is good, Red Dog answered with a smile.

I hurried back to our camp. I did not complete my part of the circling of the town, but I felt that what I had learned was important. Fox had not returned yet, so I hurried to the house of Heron and Sees Beyond.

Heron was chopping firewood near the house, using a white man's axe. Some of their tools are very useful, I have to admit. He stopped as I approached and I blurted out my news. Instantly, he was alert.

"Where is the camp of these men? You have seen it?"

"No, no, Uncle. I only talked to a man, one about my age. 'Red Dog,' he is called."

"Ah, that one," Heron mused. "Their lodge... Near a big sycamore... Yes, a hard-working young man. And, I am made to think he can be trusted."

I was amazed, that Heron would know of Red Dog and his people, but I then realized that both had lived here for some time. Of course, they would know others in the town, just as we in the Southern Band know our neighbors, even though we move often.

"How much did you tell him?"

"Nothing! We only talked a little. He told me where he lives. But he knows where White Plume is held. I thought it best not to say any more, to him."

"It is good. It would not be wise for many to know that we seek the girl. Does your father know of these things?"

"No. He has not returned yet. I hurried back."

"You did well, Badger," said Heron. "The fewer who know of your search, the better."

About then, Fox approached, heading toward our camp. I called to him and beckoned, and he changed his direction to come toward us.

Quickly, I told again my experience, in more detail this time. Sees Beyond had joined us. She said little, only listened, nodding from time to time. I had a strong feeling that her thoughts were racing, fast and true, like the flight of a falcon as it strikes a lesser bird in mid-air.

And it was good.

You may wonder why we did not ask for help from others. But, who could we ask? This was a bad situation, even in its best possibilities. We were strangers here. If such a thing had happened within the nation of the People, it would hardly be a problem at all. One of the warrior societies, probably the Bloods in our own Southern band... Maybe the Bowstrings, because that is my father's society... But, no matter. There would be a traditional way to force that which is right, to hunt down these... *Aiee*, are there words bad enough to describe these who are dung-eating excuses for men?

In most tribes and nations there are those who enforce the customs and laws of the group. It is their sworn duty to do so. Even whites, I was told, have such enforcers. They can be identified by a shiny medal pinned to their shirt, sometimes, just as our Blood Society's red paint serves the same purpose.

But, in every case, these who enforce the law have the support of their own people. A tribe, a band of a tribe; townspeople, among those who live in towns.

But there, where we were, was no one who could enforce right and wrong, or even seemed to want to do so. This town was mostly whites, who are not interested in justice for a native woman. They even show a lack of respect for their own women. So, no help could be sought there.

Among the others in the area, where could one turn? There were probably ten or more tribes or nations represented there. There was no council to make decisions, no meeting of minds, nothing.

So, anything to try to recover White Plume was up to us, with whatever help we could muster from these, our newly-found friends.

CHAPTER TWENTY-EIGHT

We had to have a plan of some sort. But, where to start? Any unusual activity that we might begin could draw the attention of White Plume's captors, and make things worse. Maybe even, deadly. We could not just go blundering into their camp, asking questions that would arouse suspicion. I suggested that possibly the father of Red Dog, might be of help. He already had some contact with the men who held White Plume. They had let him know of a girl who could be bought.

"No," advised Sees Beyond. "Let us not bring in any more people. It will be harder to plan. I am made to think that even Red Dog may be one too many."

"But his heart is good!" I protested.

"Of course!" Sees answered. "But we must keep this as simple as we can. More people, more chances for something to go wrong. Maybe his part is already finished, Badger. He has found the girl for you. Now comes someone else's part of the plan."

"But we have no plan!" said Fox.

"This is true," nodded Sees Beyond. "We need to know more before we can plan."

I was very discouraged, but I could see the danger in trying some sort of action without more than we knew at that time.

"But, how can we learn anything," Fox demanded, "without going over to their camp? We know where it is…"

"No!" Too dangerous," said Sees Beyond firmly. "But, maybe my husband can learn something more about their camp."

Heron sat thoughtfully, nodding to himself.

"How?" asked Fox, but then stopped, some embarrassment on his face. "I… uh… forgive me, Uncle. I had no…"

"It is nothing," said Heron, waving it aside. "Let us see what happens…"

Now, my friends, I do not pretend to know. There are things which one does not question. Of these, one of the most important is not to question the spirit-gifts that have been given to others. In this case, Heron's gifts could be useful. It was not for me to ask. True, I could almost convince myself that I had seen him change from a bird to a man before my eyes. Or was this only a dream-scene, brought on by my distress over White Plume? Whatever it had been, it belonged not to me, but to Heron, and one does not question another's medicine. Of course, I was making a mistake in thinking I needed to understand. Things of the spirit are mostly not to be understood, only accepted, and cherished. I was in the process of learning that.

Just then, Sees Beyond spoke, in a kindly voice. She saw that I was troubled.

"Badger," she said gently, "let Heron use his gifts."

This has been a thing of great comfort to me many times since that day. It has helped me to learn that sometimes the thing to do for a while is to wait. There are times when one may say "Don't just stand there, do something!" But it is equally important, sometimes, to accept that "Don't just do something, stand there!" is the wisdom needed. You see, I was learning patience, in a hard way.

Heron spoke again.

"Let me see what I can learn," he agreed.

I did not know how Heron proposed to use his medicine, his gifts of the spirit. Maybe, even he did not know. There are such gifts, it is said. He and Sees Beyond had entered their lodge and shut the door, with the promise that they would keep us informed.

All of this began shortly after noon, as Sun Boy paused overhead. It surely seemed a long afternoon, though I knew that Sun's journey was actually shorter than in summer.

And, so it was. I vented some of my concern and energy by cutting browse for the horses. Fox went hunting.

It was nearly dark when Sees Beyond came outside and beckoned us to come over. We hurried to their house, and entered its warmth. Heron sat near the fireplace, warming himself.

I wondered if, when one is out of body, as I suspected in these happenings, the traveling spirit feels heat or cold at all. If there is no body to be exposed to the heat of summer or the cold of winter, what does the spirit feel? To a spirit, is there any warm or cold? If not, that would be handy, no?

But there might be other things not so pleasant. A few times in my life I had seen a holy person shortly after a spirit-happening. In each of those times, there had been the appearance of complete exhaustion. A tiredness, like that following very hard work.

It was like that now, and I wondered again at the discomfort and inconvenience imposed upon those who receive the gifts of spirit. Those who are offered spirit gifts may refuse, of course, and lose the gift. But I was gaining greater respect for those who accept and use such gifts. They try to help others, at little gain to themselves, and often with inconvenience and danger.

These things were going through my mind as I watched Heron slowly recovering from the labor of his spirit-journey. I was gaining new respect for all who accept the gifts of spirit and use them for the good of others. For the first time, maybe, I was able to see the tremendous responsibility and self-denial that must be required. Maybe, even, I was growing up a little.

I had hoped that Heron's search might prove to provide the information needed to bring on some action. I was impatient, and I expected too much. This had been only a cautious look at what we would have to deal with.

"White Plume is there," Heron began. "She is not injured, and her spirit is strong. A brave woman, Fox. You must be proud. I am made to think that, in time, she could handle this herself."

Fox flushed angrily, and started to speak, but Heron quieted him with a wave of the hand.

We were all listening, waiting for whatever Heron was to tell us. It was good, that Heron seemed confident and self-assured. There are times, I suppose, that those with such gifts of the spirit must have their own doubts. It would be important not to let such doubts show. This would be only another of the problems that must confront any holy man or woman as they relate to the less-gifted of us. There must be times when one's "gift" seems more like a curse, considering the great responsibility it demands. These are things that I was just beginning to understand. Even that was in a sort of childish way. But, yes, I'll go on...

Heron, though his face showed his concern, had a look of confidence, which seemed very important to me.

"First," he began slowly, "the girl is well, and her spirit is good. Your daughter is a strong woman, Fox. I am made to think that she has managed to influence both of her captors... "

"How?" interrupted Fox. "What do you mean?"

"Well... You see how it must be. One or the other must be with her at all times, to watch her, to stop her from running away. Unless she is tied, of course. And that is too inconvenient, the tying and untying. They do so at night, mostly."

I could stand it no longer...

"Has she been raped?" I burst out.

Heron turned and looked at me for a long moment, his eyes seeing into my very thoughts. There was a trace of pity, but mostly a feeling of understanding and sympathy.

He knew my concerns. I had tried to console myself with the thought that she would have brought a better price if she were not violated, but I knew that this was a slim hope, at best. I would love her anyway, no matter what had happened to her.

"Badger," the seer finally said, in a kindly tone," I understand your worries. It would be hard to think of her suffering, but it would not make a difference to you beyond that, would it? Would you love her any less?"

He went on, without waiting for an answer.

"I was able to see into her head, some. Part of this, I am guessing, but this will be close to how it has been. First, White Plume will have found ways to make them distrust each other. She would, a great part of the time, be with one or the other. During that time, she would be able to make that one think she fears the other... 'He makes me afraid.' This causes distrust between them. They know each other as untrustworthy from the start. This is what has brought them together, no? So this brings each to want to tell the girl 'Do not fear him, I will protect you!'"

This brought me to the thought that both would expect her favors, but before I could question, Heron lifted a hand to stop me.

"Ah, I see where your thought is going, Badger. Now she will owe something to both? But remember, she is a woman."

This confused me for a moment, but then I began to see. Among the People, a woman's "moon time" is her own. During that week she must not touch any cooking things, or any weapons. Some of the other tribes even have a "moon lodge" where the menstruating women spend that week, no? It is safest. I have learned that whites do not understand this, and consider this unfair to the woman. They miss the main point, that the menstrual lodge at the edge of the camp gives the woman power. She decides when it is time to stay away from the cooking, skinning, tanning, and other duties as a wife. Only she knows, for sure...

"I am made to think," Heron went on, "that White Plume has played the part of a woman. Only she knows. It is possible, even, that she would convince her captors that her moon time has been thrown off schedule by her abuse, and is now all wrong.

"But, would that make a difference to these men?" asked Fox. "We can see what kind they are."

"We don't know," admitted Heron. "I am only speaking of what a wise young woman might have done."

"Are these white men?" asked Fox. "That may make a difference."

"Yes, it could," Heron agreed, "but, my friend, this sort of man gives a bad name to all men. Among your people, mine, whites... Everywhere, there must be some of these. Our people would drive them out. Probably, yours would, too. Maybe, even the whites would. So, it matters little who they are, when we know what they are. And, this gives us an advantage. It can be used against them, their lack of morals. They probably do not even trust each other. This is why I am made to think a clever young woman can outwit them, convince each to protect her from the other, no?"

This was a long speech for Heron, who usually was not inclined to voice more than a few words. But now he went on.

"Next, we must make contact."

"But you..." Fox began, but stopped quickly, realizing that Heron's contact had not been a physical one. Possibly, even, it could have gone unnoticed. Of such things, one does not ask.

"Now," Heron went on, "I can approach them in body."

Yes, my guess had been right, I noted. Heron had been in their camp in spirit only. But now...

"These men have seen Sees Beyond and me from time to time. They know we are camped somewhere near, and that we visit the spring for water. So, one of us must make the contact."

I was beginning to see where this was going. It would be a matter of who would make the contact, Heron or Sees Beyond. If either I or Fox approached their camp, White Plume's reaction might get any or all of us killed.

Her captors had already let it be known that they had a woman for sale or trade. Red Dog had given us that information. So, it would be logical for anyone with an interest to inquire, no? And, it would be unwise to bring in more people, we had agreed.

Heron went on to explain what he had in mind. It would not be seemly for a woman to make the advance, so Heron suggested that he approach White Plume's captors. Heron's story would be that he was in need of a young woman to help his wife with household chores.

Sees Beyond gave a snort of disapproval that anyone might think such a thing, but Heron continued.

"They have seen both of us, and will believe such a thing. While we argue about the price, I will learn all I can about how the girl is treated, and the best way to free her."

We talked about this for a little while, and even the possibility of buying White Plume's freedom. That did not seem to be a good plan, since we really had little to trade, except for the horses. No, this would be a contact for information, only. The planning would come next.

"I will go over in the morning," Heron suggested. "I will tell them that I heard from one of the men nearby that they have a woman to sell or trade. That much is true, no?"

It was a place to start...

CHAPTER TWENTY-NINE

Now, as I am telling you this, you must remember that it was not easy. We still had some trouble with language, but what we needed seemed always to be there. The mix of several tongues, along with hand signs, seemed to lead to the exchange of ideas when we tried. Sometimes there would be a moment of confusion, which might be cleared away in a heartbeat by a chance remark of any one of the four of us. As Heron had noted, "The spirits have a sense of humor."

It helped a great deal, also, to have Sees Beyond with us. As a woman, she was sensitive to what a captive girl might be experiencing. She and Heron had had two babies, we learned, but both had died when they were small.

"It was not to be," explained Sees. "It was meant that we were to use our spirit-gifts in other ways. Maybe, with such problems as yours, here. But, sometimes I almost wish that I had refused the gift. To hold a baby... *Aiee*, what am I thinking? Let us work on the task before us, here!"

But now I am rambling. Forgive me, friends.

We needed a plan, badly, and Sees Beyond seemed to be the one to feel the moods of others. Maybe this is a gift given mostly to women. I don't know. But it did help to have Sees interpret for us how the captive White Plume might be thinking.

"We must make a contact," she said thoughtfully. "It would be too risky for either Fox or Badger, here, to walk into their camp. The girl's reaction, we can't guess. I should be the one to go."

Heron started to speak, but she stopped him, as if he had not come up with a plan at all.

"No, I have seen these two at the spring, a time or two. They have seen me, and will remember me as a harmless old woman, no? Hardly worth noticing, but not dangerous to them."

"They would not see me as dangerous," protested Heron with a chuckle.

"True. But you are a man. They would be trying to guess what your interest in the girl would be. My purpose, they will assume, is simply to look after another woman's problems. They will send me away, but I will have learned more in a short time than any man could, even Heron. Is it not so?"

We all had to agree.

"I will carry a waterskin," Sees Beyond was saying.

Apparently she had thought out her whole plan already. We had to admit, it was a better plan than Heron's, though it was based on the same approach: A slave-girl to help Sees Beyond with her "women's work."

As if that thought had been in the woman's mind, she began to explain.

"I can ask about the girl. Not whether they have one, but that I have heard so. I will be looking for a girl to help me with my daily tasks, now that I am getting old and feeble."

I almost smiled at that. Of all the words that might have been chosen to indicate anything about Sees Beyond, those would not even have been considered.

Heron chuckled.

"Yes, you can tell them how your husband beats you because you can't get your work done."

I was confused.

This seemed to make no sense, until I realized that this couple were teasing each other. They were friends, who shared their problems. Even among the People, I had rarely seen such understanding. Maybe it was that Heron and Sees, with no children, were made to spend more time alone together. But, who knows? Yes, I will go on.

"I will do this," Sees was saying. "I will fill my waterskin, and stop by their camp, obviously tired, to ask about the girl on my way back. That will make it look good."

Fox was a bit doubtful.

"Is this safe, Mother?"

"Of course," she responded quickly, pausing with a smile, "unless you mean for them! That is another matter."

Heron said nothing, but chuckled quietly. I got the idea that there were things he could have told.

We learned later, the details of Sees' visit to the camp of the two men. She had filled the waterskin, and pretending to limp, staggered into their clearing. She set down her burden and turned to the two men, completely ignoring the girl.

Now, I have to describe their place, as Sees Beyond told it to us. There was a small canvas tent, like our lean-to, with a fire in front of the opening. Not a good fire, useful for heat, but too big, of course. A white man's fire. The tent was much like ours, Fox's and mine.

White Plume could be seen inside, awake and alert. That part was good news. She was tied by a rope around her waist, the knot in back, where she could not reach it. It was kept there, Sees explained, by a shorter thong around each shoulder, linked to one around the neck. Sees Beyond was given the thought that these men were familiar with this sort of thing. Maybe, even, it was their way, as Fox's was that of a trader. We did not know whether to think of this as good or bad. It would be to their advantage to treat such a prisoner well, to increase her value. Still, *Aiee*, I was suffering with concern for White Plume.

"She does well," Sees assured us. "A clever girl. She has managed to play one against the other. Not too much... If they fight, the stronger would assume that he won her, which would not be good."

"Did you let her know that we are here?" demanded Fox.

"No, I thought that too risky, too much to add to her burden just now. But she knows that I am here, and will help her."

"How did you do that?" asked Heron.

The woman chuckled.

"I told her that my husband is a thankless, lazy no-good who beats me and always demands more than I can do."

"So, I am the bad one?" Heron protested with a smile.

"I want the men to think so," Sees went on. "More like themselves. But she knows better. She smiled."

"*Aiee!*" Heron teased. "How do you women do that?"

"Oh, just a nod, a smile. A sideways glance."

"That is true," Fox interrupted. "There is some of that in trading."

"Yes," agreed Heron. "I have noticed this. I never thought much about it. But now... Mother, would you say now that our White Plume knows we are here?"

"Maybe not," said Sees Beyond in a kindly tone. "She knows that something is moving. She will be ready for anything, and ready to help when the moment comes."

"So, old woman," said Heron with a smile, "for now I am to be the rough, non-understanding, poor excuse for a husband, who probably beats his wife and complains about her cooking."

"That is your description, not mine," taunted Sees Beyond. "If the moccasin fits... But let us eat and plan our next steps."

CHAPTER THIRTY

This part, of course, is how Sees Beyond told us later, after she returned with her waterskin. She had learned much. As we would expect, one of the men who held White Plume captive was a leader, bullying the other a little bit all the time, just to keep it that way. Is it not always so? The leader also rations out privileges to the lesser member or members, to keep their interest and loyalty. In this case, just the one companion.

I could hardly bear to think of what the promised privileges might be, in this situation. Time alone with the female prisoner? I began to imagine what I would do to either of these men if they harmed White Plume. I knew it was a foolish, childish thing to create in my head... Painful tortures to some of the more sensitive parts of their bodies. But, ah, no worse than the torture I was living through, worrying about the woman I loved.

Sees Beyond had done her work well, scouting the enemy camp. She had managed to learn much about the kidnapers. Who was the leader, which the follower? The big one with a heavy black beard had appeared more dangerous at first, but she had quickly realized that this was an error. The leader was the other, a slim, weasely-looking man of middle age.

Sees had also scouted out their horses. It would help to know how well-mounted the enemy might be. There were two riding horses and two pack animals. One, "the kind with big ears," Sees Beyond added to the description. Apparently, as they traveled, White Plume had ridden one of the pack horses. Probably she had been tied to the animal.

"Now, let us plan," the seer went on.

Quickly, she sketched out her ideas. It would be best, she had decided, for her to return with Heron to bargain with the renegades. Possibly, more than once. If the captors of White Plume became accustomed to the coming and going of the older couple, they would become careless and inattentive.

"We might even argue between us," Sees suggested. "That would make us seem to them just a harmless old couple, not very wise."

"It is good," agreed Heron with a wry smile. "Only, not too stupid, no?"

Mischief sparkled in her eyes.

"We will see!" she chided.

Again, I was impressed that here was a couple who understood and trusted each other. Enjoyed each other as friends, as well as partners and lovers. There was always this light-hearted teasing, even in the most threatening situations.

Understand, though... There was no neglect of how serious our problem was. It would take some planning. When our plan of action began, it would be up to each of the four of us to be ready and able to carry out our part.

For now, Sees and Heron would make a visit, together, arguing as they tried to bargain for the girl.

It was growing dark, and this next move would not be until morning. I had another restless night.

I have to pause once again to say what a remarkable couple these two proved to be. It would have been so easy for Sees and

Heron to choose not to help us, even threatening us if we persisted. I could not imagine either of them as a threatening person, yet it must be understood that the medicine of either one was powerful enough to be very dangerous. And again, I noted the great responsibility that is thrust upon those who have such gifts. It is no wonder that many refuse the spirit-gift because of the responsibility involved.

But, enough... Sees Beyond told us later, how the visit went. They approached the camp of the woman-stealers, arguing a little to distract the men.

"I need someone who is young and strong," Sees Beyond told the men. "This husband of mine is lazy and worthless."

"You do not have to bring that into the trading," Heron observed, with a wry face.

You see, if the two men became amused at the arguing couple, it would weaken their attention. And these two could play it to the hilt. I do not know what tongue they were using. Both were skilled in several languages, and we could be sure that for this occasion they chose to argue in a tongue that could be easily understood by the woman-stealers.

"True," Sees responded, "but I must point out to them how desperate my need is."

"And what of my need?" Heron responded.

"Your need?" the medicine woman snapped back. "This is to be a helper for me, not a playmate for an old buck like you."

"Old buck? Ha!" Heron snorted.

By this time the kidnapers were laughing, thoroughly off guard.

"Now, now, don't fight, children," pleaded the leader, between spasms of laughter. "Do we have trading to discuss, or not? What do you have to offer for this fine young slave?"

"Nothing, yet," snapped Sees Beyond. "I have not even seen this woman, except at a distance. How do I know whether she can do the work I need done? I want to see her, talk to her. Is that not fair?"

"Of course, of course, Mother," said the black-bearded one.

"Let me do this trading," snapped the other of the two, the leader, with some irritation.

He spoke in the white man's tongue, probably thinking it would not be known to Sees and Heron. He was wrong about that, too, of course.

"Let me look at her," Sees Beyond insisted. "Bring her out where I can see her. I can't use a weakling!"

"Oh-keh, Mother," the leader said. "As you wish!"

He was laughing, which was good. It would be easier, because he was to be off guard. That, of course, was the purpose of the entire situation.

White Plume was led out of the small lean-to, a thong or light rope around her right ankle, to prevent any attempt at escape. It appeared that she wore this tether at all times. The other end would be tied to a tree or maybe to the other part of the shelter, to signal any attempt to escape. I don't know, exactly, but this is as Sees Beyond saw it and told us later.

The ankle where the rope was tied was rubbed raw. I learned that only later, of course, but Sees Beyond drew down on that at once.

"What is this?" she demanded. "You said the girl is in good condition! This one is thin, half crippled from that cursed rope. What are you trying to do, trading damaged goods? I may be old, but I am not stupid!"

All of this was overplayed, of course, as a part of a potential trade. At least, that was what the girl's captors were to believe. It would also provide an opportunity to let the girl know how the situation stood. In that, they must be very cautious. If her face, or even the way she stood or moved, gave any clue to an escape plan, she might be as good as dead.

Now, Sees Beyond faced the girl again, her back to the men, feet braced apart and her hands on hips. In the fading evening light, her body and clothing blocked the view of the girl from the others, at least partly. Sees was muttering to herself. But in front of her, her hands and her facial expression were busy, largely unnoticed by the girl's captors.

"Damaged goods?" she mumbled aloud. "I don't know... Maybe she is strong enough, though... I must think on it."

The message that the girl was receiving was different:

Do not react. We are here to help. We will return.

The girl nodded, very slightly, burst into tears, and turned back into the shelter in the fading light.

CHAPTER THIRTY-ONE

Now would come the time to plan the rescue in detail. There was still a certain amount of danger in any attempt.

It was tempting to think about a well-placed arrow, loosed from concealment in the woods. But, that would be very dangerous. A miss, after all, would be a possibility. That would alert the enemy, and could even cause them to harm White Plume.

Even if an arrow found its mark, there would be the other man to contend with. And, if it happened that way, who would predict what the surviving scoundrel might choose to do? He might kill the prisoner.

Two arrows, loosed at once? Another possibility. But again, both arrows must arrive at nearly the same moment, having been launched exactly together. And, both with accuracy, of course.

We kept coming back to the same point; one or the other of the men must be somehow removed from the plan for the other's fate. Shoot one, maybe, while the other was absent. We began to look on this plan with some favor.

How should it be? Shoot the one who was away from the camp, or the watchdog, and then the other when he returned?

We agreed that the leader was clever enough to be dangerous, but that the large hair-faced one would be the hardest to put down.

"I am made to think," said Sees Beyond thoughtfully, "that the one with not so much fur on his face is the more dangerous. The other, strong as a bull, but a little bit slow."

Maybe, Heron suggested, it could be that they visit again as a couple, squabbling a little. That had seemed to amuse the two men, especially the leader. To keep that one off guard would help greatly.

"If they become used to seeing us, they will not pay so much attention," Heron went on. "We must not string it out too long, but if they see us more, they may begin to be careless."

"It is good," agreed Sees Beyond. "But we must not push it too far. They might become suspicious. They might also find someone else who wants to trade for a young woman."

My heart was heavy, of course, to hear them talk of my White Plume, my love, in this way, like something for sale or trade. Maybe it was good, though, for me to see that this was actually how most strangers would see it. This made me think again of poor Fox. My White Plume was his daughter, and I had no way to understand how much he must be suffering.

Now, it was very hard for me, of course. As a young man in love, I was certain that no one in all of time had ever felt such love as this. I was ready to explode like the flash in the pan of the white man's gun when the striker makes its spark. But I also knew that to be too impatient could be very dangerous to White Plume.

I did have the comfort that the mysterious couple who had become our friends had powerful medicine. That would seem to have made things very simple. But, it was easy to misjudge the strength of such a gift, as well as its use. I do not pretend to understand such medicine, but I was learning. As I have said, such a gift carries with it a very heavy burden. If it is misused, there is great danger. Medicine such as that of Sees Beyond, if used to harm anyone, could turn the harm onto the user. Misuse could be fatal. *Aiee,* how could one tell? What might seem helpful and good, to destroy an evil enemy, might be a mis-understanding. Also, I suspect that such a misuse of the gift might be possible only at the sacrifice of the seer's life. There are such stories among the People... A holy man who used his gift to kill a traitor among the People, knowing that to do so, he must sacrifice his own life.

I was reminded of the Death Song of the People, traditionally used as they rode into battle, especially when hopelessly outnumbered.

"The Earth and the Sky go on forever, but today is a good day to die."

I had always thought, boastfully, that I would be proud to sing the Death Song as a warrior of the People. And yes, I still thought that I could do that if I needed to, if it would save the woman I loved.

But, it was at that point that my doubts began to bubble up inside me. Not whether I could die to save White Plume, but... Would my sacrifice actually save her? What if I died in the effort, and they killed her anyway? Or, after killing me, Fox, and maybe Heron, they were still able to sell White Plume into a fate that I did not want to think about. Finally, I came to a decision. Yes, I could give my life for hers, if I must. Not to have tried, and to survive, myself, while White Plume remained a captive, a thing for sale or trade, would be a thing of shame for all my days. I could not live with that. I must try, at my own risk.

Of course, I said nothing to the others. Heron and Sees Beyond were the ones to make the plans, along with Fox. I could only resolve to carry out whatever task they assigned to me. And of course, we had come to trust the holy couple.

Now that I think on it, I do not recall another such husband-wife pair. Both had spirit gifts, powerful in different ways, but useful in their differences, no?

"Maybe," suggested Heron, "when we go back we could muddy the water a little, bring in more to the trade."

"What do you mean?" asked Fox.

"Insist on something else from them. Maybe a horse to transport the woman we're buying."

"But there is no need..." began Fox.

"Of course not," smiled Sees Beyond, who quickly understood her partner. "But, it gives us more space to argue. Something we can back down on, and they will think they won something."

"Yes," agreed Fox. "I should have thought of it, as a trader. But this trade is too close to me."

Heron nodded sympathetically. "That is true. But, it will also give us a chance to look at their horses more closely, as a part of a trade. Even if we don't trade, as we probably will not, we will know about how well they may be equipped for any pursuit when you start back to your family."

It was a long speech for Heron, but very meaningful. To add one more bit of confusion into the matter... The black-bearded one, who may have been confused anyway... Well, you get the idea.

"Maybe we could barter for the horse," suggested Fox. "They need not know that we have been in contact."

"No," Sees Beyond shook her head. "That would quickly confuse things. We must keep it simple. I know, you are restless, you want to help. But your help, for now, is to stay out of sight. They think they are trading with a simple-minded old couple who fight and argue between us. Besides, having a woman taking part in the trade will help the girl."

There was no denying that, of course.

"That is true," agreed Heron, "but let me think on this. These two are not the most clever. Anything to distract, or even amuse them... "

"Yes," agreed his wife. "We are already using that. I have scolded you for wanting to buy a fine-looking young woman."

"I saw that," Heron answered. "You did not have to call me a 'bull in the rutting season.'"

I was beginning to understand their approach. Heron would push toward completing the bargain. His wife would retaliate, pretending to be angry at his urgency to acquire a young woman, apparently for his own male pleasure. Such a thought made my heart very heavy. I could easily have lost my temper over this. I had to see it as a part of the rescue effort, without allowing myself to think of failure. I was ready to kill, I told myself.

I had grown up as a young man of the People, expecting to see battle at some time. Many strangers from other places had been moving in from the east. Whites, and other tribes. Yet, our story skins show that even in times long ago, we fought with others. Our allies, the Head Splitters, were once the enemy, it is said. We became brothers only because a greater enemy threatened both.

It has always been so, I suppose. A man becomes a man by counting coup in combat, which requires a certain willingness to die, rather than surrender. I was sure that I could do so if need arose. White Plume would cry in mourning, in my honor, which would be a good thing. I had not yet realized that I would be present only in spirit if I died, even with honor.

I am made to think that there comes a time in the life of every young person, when we come to realize that we are not immortal. On any day since birth, there might be the possibility, through accident or illness or war, that we might cross over to the Other Side.

Even so, I knew, as I still know, that I was willing to die for White Plume, to shelter her from harm. Again, I promised myself that I would do nothing that would put White Plume into any more danger than that which now hovered over her. I must trust the planning of the holy couple and their powerful medicine.

CHAPTER THIRTY-TWO

I have not mentioned the shaking of the earth for a little while. Was the earth still shaking? Oh, yes, but just a little bit. It seems odd, now, that we could look back, and think that if earth shakes only a little bit, it does not matter much. We can become accustomed to nearly anything, it seems. Now, the shaking of the earth was not nearly so important as the rescue of White Plume. Something must happen, and soon.

It was then that I heard the owl. There was something unusual about it that caused me to pause and listen carefully. In autumn, of course, it is common to see and hear the great hunting owl near sunset. There are many different kinds of owls, but we see the one with ears like horns most often, and in autumn. Our people have always respected this hunter-brother. His hunting call is his name: "Kookooskoos." Others have similar calls, but that of Kookooskoos is unmistakable, no?

I had been told that this hunter may be found almost anywhere. White Plume's family had traveled a lot, and we had talked of this before, when her brother, Toad, killed the owl.

This still bothered me. I wondered, even, if the capture of White Plume might be a result of her brother's actions.

No, I decided, it would not seem so. Their relationship to Kookooskoos was different from mine. I had seen White Plume's brother kill an owl for what I considered no good reason, and I had been offended. Was this in any way connected? I could not see it so. Among their people, the owl does not have the respect that our People give this fellow hunter.

This was becoming confusing to me, that my thoughts had been turned to Toad. Was there a message here that I was not understanding? The owl called again, and another answered from the heavier timber to the west. I decided not to worry about it. It had been only a passing thought.

But it was not easy to push these thoughts aside. I did not hear the owl again, beyond three calls, yet my head kept telling me that this was important.

Heron and Sees set out as they had planned, prepared to haggle. They took a pack horse as a possible trade item. This was somewhat risky. The two trappers might even recognize the animal from back along the trail. But, trades were frequent, especially at this time of year. This would simply suggest a real desire to trade. At least, we hoped so.

The waiting was the hardest, of course. I walked back and forth until I realized that it was bothering Fox, and I came back to sit and wait some more. Finally, Fox spoke.

"Go ahead and take a walk. I will come and tell you when they return."

It seemed like a good idea. I was useless there. Maybe I could hunt a little. I took my bow and three arrows, and pointed my direction.

"Toward the river."

It is good, Fox signed. He was probably weary of watching me fidget.

I was in no mood, of course, to do any serious hunting. This was only an escape from the waiting, which was really no escape at all. In addition, with so many people camped in the area because of the damage caused by the shaking earth... Well, I had to be doing something.

I have tried to tell myself that it was only a mistake, a loss of direction, which brought me near the camp of the Bad Ones. Maybe so. Maybe I wanted to be of help so badly that I made such a mistake. Or maybe I was guided.

I had not had much experience in heavy woods such as this, having grown up in the tallgrass prairie. In addition to that, the sky was overcast, the wind was still, and every tree looks much like another tree, no? Yes,

I am a child of the open prairie.

What? Yes, it could have been that this was partly as I would have it, to make excuse for my stupidity, but maybe... Let me go on...

I found myself looking at a campsite from the back side, so to speak. It did not take long to understand that, by accident or guidance or whatever forces were at work, here was the camp of the men who held White Plume. I could see the one with heavy black fur on his face.

As quickly as I could, I ducked aside and out of sight. I could hear voices... One, a woman's voice, which I recognized as that of Sees Beyond. The tones rose and fell, those of an argument over a trade. That, I supposed, was to the good, but I could not hear what was being said.

I knew that I had no excuse for being here. I could easily destroy the chance for White Plume's rescue. Carefully, I backed away. My heart was heavy as I did so, but there was no other way.

As I retreated through the pines and cedars, I caught a glimpse of the people in the camp. There was much talk, which

I could not hear, and much gesturing and pointing to the pack horse that Heron had taken along.

I was not certain, but it appeared that there was an extra man, one whom I had not seen before. He seemed to be holding another horse. I had not seen that horse before, either.

This was bad news, another to trade. My heart was very heavy as I slipped away, hoping that Heron and Sees Beyond would use all of their skills in this new and unexpected situation, the three-cornered bartering game.

As I turned, I was surprised to see a man I had not noticed before. A stupid mistake on my part, of course. I had been busy looking at the camp of the Bad Ones, instead of making sure of my own safety.

There, behind me, was a man with the black fur on his face, no more than a few steps away, watching me. *Aiee*, he could have killed me before I knew he was there.

But, had I not seen him in their camp only a short time ago? My friends, I had made a bad mistake, one that could have cost my life. Yes, I had seen such a man in their camp. I had not thought about one possibility: There might be more than one of the men with the black fur on their faces. And, as we know, all white men look pretty much alike. Was this the man we had seen, or another, and more seriously, were there three men involved in the capture and captivity of White Plume, instead of two?

Or, was this man another, not even connected in any way with what was going on?

I had to decide quickly what I must do. I carried weapons which anyone in the area would see as ordinary hunting tools, and I quickly decided to act as if that was my purpose. I nodded to him and changed the direction of my motion, as if to continue my hunt without bothering his hunt.

It was almost a surprise when the other man nodded in return and changed his direction, also, so as not to bother my hunt. Still, it was a dangerous situation. We watched each other closely as we drew apart. Neither of us was ready to trust the other, in such a meeting. In this way, we separated, and moved on.

CHAPTER THIRTY-THREE

But I still had doubts and fears. I was confused. I felt that I was missing something. I could not shake the idea that it was intended that I see a message of some sort in the encounters with this other man, or with the owls. If nothing else, maybe just a reminder that customs are different.

I was wishing that I felt more comfortable in talking with Heron or Sees Beyond. Maybe they could help me, and to explain the feelings that I had about the owls. But among the People, I have grown up with the constant warning: "Don't bother the holy persons!" They are busy constantly in their minds, with visions and warnings and interpretations. They have no time to answer the questions of a child, I was always told.

I had just begun to realize, since our close contact with Heron and Sees, that holy people are people. They can be happy or sad, hungry or full, tired or refreshed, like the rest of us. Close behind such thoughts as that came a recognition that theirs is a heavy responsibility. I have been told that among some tribes, as many as half are born with the gifts of the spirit, the "medicine." They can refuse it, and the responsibility is lifted. But, the gift would be lost, of course.

There is also the matter of misuse of such a gift. If it is used for personal gain or to hurt others, it may turn the hurt on the user. Among the People, we recall the legend of a great Holy Man who used his medicine to kill a traitor in his own band. It seemed the only way to protect the People, and it was successful. But within days, that holy man himself was dead. Knowing of this danger, he had sacrificed himself for the rest of us, because it had seemed the only way.

I had no way of knowing the customs and traditions of Sees and Heron, but I was afraid for them, in that they might be caught in such a trap. I hoped and prayed not, but oh, how important it was to me that White Plume be recovered from the Bad Ones.

I worked my way around through the woods, still uneasy, not to be able to see farther than a few steps. This was no setting in which a child of our prairie country could be comfortable. Even with the trees still nearly bare, except for the pines and cedars, I could not see far enough to really feel good about it.

I saw a movement through the trees, and moved my head, carefully, of course, to see what it might be. An animal, of a color that would probably be a deer. Their color varies, of course, from reddish to yellow, but often a gray. This one would be in winter hair, and that, too, I had learned could be different from another deer of the same kind.

It was good that I was cautious, and that I moved slowly. It took me a few heartbeats to realize that there was more than one problem. I was too close to the camp of the bad men to even try for a kill. I would have to let this opportunity slip past. There was much more at stake than a deer kill.

An even greater problem rose a moment later. The animal stepped from behind a brushy cedar, and I saw that it was not a deer at all, but a horse. Not a real horse, but the rabbit-ears horse used as a pack animal by the whites. I have mentioned that Fox used one of these, to pack trade goods. A "mule," I have told you it is called. They are said to be more sensible than a horse. Fox always said that while a horse may overeat and cause stomach problems, given such a chance, the mule understands this, and avoids these problems. It is also said that the mule tends to be stubborn. This is not true, says Fox. If the mule refuses to do what is asked, there is a reason. The saddle may be rubbing a sore on his hide, or he may have a thorn or a stone in a foot, that will cause him to go lame.

A horse, in such a situation, may continue with his task until he goes lame, or produces a festering wound. Not the mule. We must find the reason for mule's refusal, or we may find ourselves carrying his load. At least, Fox said so.

So many things had happened since those autumn days that I could not completely recall... But, this rabbit-ears had a familiar look about it. Are they all the same color? I did not know. And, at the time White Plume had been stolen, had the Bad Ones not also taken a horse?

Not that it would make any difference at this time, except to mark the thieves as even more evil. In the prairie, the loss of a horse could be fatal. To steal a horse might put a man on foot in a dangerous position, unable to travel to the nearest source of water, maybe a day's travel away. This would not be as much a problem here, but I am a child of the plains, and my feelings reacted this way. These were truly evil men. Just another thing about them for me to hate.

It was just then that the pack animal stepped on out into the open clearing. Now I was certain. Yes, this was Fox's pack animal. It must have been stolen at the same time as White Plume was carried off.

How could it be that we had not noticed this? I was puzzled, but then, when I thought... Fox and I had been forced to avoid being seen. The facts that we had about the Bad Ones were from what we had gathered by tracking, and from what we were told by Heron and Sees Beyond. Neither Fox nor I had been able to watch them closely. Heron and Sees could not recognize this animal as Fox's.

As I have said, I was impatient in these surroundings. I have never overcome the feeling that I have in a heavy growth of trees and brush. How can people live in a place where they cannot even see the horizon, and the rising and setting of the sun, the moon and the stars at night? That is also how I feel when looking into a cave, not knowing what may be lying in wait in the darkness. It was like that. I know, some will laugh at this. Some even live in caves, or in holes dug into the ground, like the Growers in our country. I have been in some of those lodges when we sometimes trade with them after the buffalo hunt, and felt that I was gasping for air as the walls closed in. *Aiee!*

What? Oh, yes. I will go on. Forgive me. I was only trying to explain how I often felt in that heavily-treed country. This is a part of the story. Even having wintered there, and becoming more familiar with what to expect had not really taught me to tolerate it any better.

I had been watching the animal through the brush and tangle of leafless branches, at times hidden by a clump of cedar or pines. I was actually off balance because I had stopped in mid-stride. I was preparing to move into a better position, when the mule took another step or two forward, to more easily reach a clump of willow or cottonwood that appeared favorable to browsing.

It was only then that I was able to see that the animal was led by the man in buckskins. He had been standing and walking on the other side, beyond the browsing animal from where I stood. Now, I must not move a muscle, even at this awkward angle. Motion would surely catch the eye of the man. Maybe he had already seen me, from behind the mule.

The brush was thick and more so with the swelling buds, so that my view was not good at all. I could only hope that the difficulty I was having was also making it hard to see me. It was just then that Kookooskoos gave his hollow cry, from a perch in a tall cottonwood near the place the mule browsed contentedly.

"Thank you, Grandfather!" I thought silently.

Because, apparently startled by the call, the man took a step which brought him into the open, where I could easily see him. It was, as I had expected, one of the trappers, one with black fur on his face.

Now, I was puzzled for a moment. Did they suspect that we had followed them all this time? Or, were they holding the mule as an unknown trade item to surprise those who might seriously want to trade, after the nit-picking part of the trade began? There was even some doubt in the back of my mind, whether this man was one of White Plume's captors at all, or just another trapper.

Meanwhile, you can imagine how I felt, unable to do anything but watch at a distance, trying not to be seen.

So far, I believed, I had not. But, I dared not move.

It was possible, though, that I had been seen. There was nothing to gain in trying to hide. It would only arouse suspicion.

I raised a hand, slowly, as if to sign that I respected the other's space to hunt or find browse for his horse, or anything else he was doing.

"It is good," I signed.

This was my effort to say "I will not bother your hunt." This was about all that I could have said or done in this situation, no?

I moved slowly, watched by the other man. I made no effort to stay out of sight, because that would draw his attention. If this was successful, I would seem only a harmless young man on a hunt. It was the best I could do under the circumstances. His eyes followed me, at every step.

What? How far away? Maybe a long bowshot. But I needed to stay in the open, so that I would appear to be only another hunter. If I ducked behind the bushes and scrubby trees, the man would become suspicious, no?

It seemed to take a long time to cross that clearing while the man watched. As I neared a thicket which would hide his view of me, I turned, looked at him slowly and deliberately, and carefully repeated the hand sign, "It is good."

The man seemed to nod, or maybe I only hoped so, as I moved on.

What now? I had apparently made a discovery, that of the pack mule, but I could not be absolutely certain that it was the same animal. To me, one mule looks much like another. I had not seen many. The next puzzling question was much more serious: Was this man the same as the hairy-faced white man at the camp where White Plume was being held? I could not be sure. They, too, all look alike.

Maybe, in his adult wisdom, Fox would be able to bring some thinking that, so far, I had not been able to see. Yes, that would be best...

CHAPTER THIRTY-FOUR

"You talked with this man?" Fox demanded.

"Only by hand signs," I assured him. "I could not just do nothing, so I pretended to be hunting."

Fox nodded thoughtfully.

"You did well, I am made to think," he pondered. "You did not see Heron and Sees Beyond?"

"No. I was trying not to stumble into the camp."

"It is good," he nodded in approval. "Now, we wait."

It was not long, though, that Fox turned to me again.

"You said the hunter you saw had a mule?"

"Yes... It seemed so. Long ears, yellow-brown in color. It reminded me of your pack animal."

"It could be," he pondered. "They could have stolen him to carry some of their packs, or to have an extra mount to ride. We were busy thinking about White Plume, not about pack animals. Then, as we traveled, we were not looking for an extra animal or its tracks, but for the broken twigs White Plume was using to mark the trail for us. But, they could have stolen or traded for a mule since they came here, no?"

"That is true," I agreed. "And, as I said, I was not sure that this white man was with them, even. Maybe his camp is near."

Again, we must sit and wait, and that was hardest of all.

It was late in the day when Sees Beyond and Heron returned to our camp.

"They are hard to deal with," Heron said. "Fox, your daughter is a fine young woman, and these men know her worth in any trade."

I wanted to ask about the mule, and to learn how this extra man fit into the story, but this did not seem to be the time for it. Maybe, even, there was no connection at all. Yet, I felt, somehow, that in some way, there was, if I could just understand the importance of it. *Aiee*, it was a worrisome day!

"They are looking for some extra value," Heron explained. "Have you anything more to trade?"

"Not here," Fox replied. "We had not thought to trade, but to rescue."

Heron nodded thoughtfully.

"I understand. But here, you are in their country, and the girl in their camp."

"Do you see anyone else trying to trade with them?" asked Fox.

"Not seriously," said Heron. "Some are curious. Your daughter is, of course, a very attractive woman."

There was again an unpleasant silence for a little while. No one wanted to follow that thought very far.

Now, you have to understand one more thing which could be very important. We were in the country of the whites. In our own territory, what is right or wrong is set by the ways of our People. If we are in the land of our neighbors... the Kenza, maybe... It is better to respect their ways than to offend them.

We could, of course, but we might want to trade with them. Buy vegetables from them, or trade meat and hides for things they grow. So, when we camp in the territory of others, it is best to go by their ways, when we can, no? We know the customs of our neighbors, and how to avoid offending them.

With whites, it is a different matter. Some seem to have no honesty at all, and kill and steal with no thought about it. Others seem to deal well among themselves, but have no hesitation to steal from anyone else. Still others respect the ways and customs of those they deal with.

We really had no knowledge of the people in this town. Maybe, even, it was not even a town at all. Maybe it was just a place where many people landed because of the shaking earth, and still happened to be there when it stopped moving.

Actually, we were not even sure of that. But, there had been very little shaking for some time. The river, which had run backward for several days, had stopped, changed again, and then resumed its normal flow. Such things no longer bothered us. Maybe the prolonged Moon of Madness was over. But how could we tell? We had nothing to compare.

The people who were there when winter came had been there for the winter, it seemed, though some may have moved on by this time. We had thought that it was a town or settlement of the whites. There was no way to know, though, whether they had any council or warrior society whose duty it was to enforce the rules. If, actually, there were any rules. Even that would be hard to tell, in a camp of whites. We had to depend on the judgment of Heron and Sees Beyond, as well as their medicine.

It was possible, even, that this was a native town of people crowded out by the whites farther east. But no, Cherokees or Creeks or Choctaws were well-organized and governed, and we had seen no signs of any such authority here. We must depend on our own actions.

There was one other thing that day, when Heron and Sees returned to their house that evening. At the time, it did not seem important.

When Fox mentioned my encounter with the hairface who was leading a mule, Heron nodded.

"That is one of the two," he explained. "The other is the leader, and the one you saw is not as wise. He does what his leader says. It is good that you made no more contact with him, Badger. It will be best to avoid him."

Heron was very gentle with his words. I did not deserve such a kind reaction. It was still possible that my chance encounter would destroy all possibility of rescuing White Plume by trade or bargain, if these woman-stealers realized our connection.

CHAPTER THIRTY-FIVE

Fox and I were impatient to ask the medicine couple what was to come next, but we knew it was best to wait. We had come to trust their advice, and knew that we would have been helpless without them. In that we had been very fortunate.

But back to my story. There was still much that we did not know. I was still confused as to how many white men were in that camp, since they all look alike.

When Heron and Sees Beyond returned to their house, they beckoned us over. We exchanged our information. "You talked to the man?" Heron blurted, as I told my story.

"No, no!" I told them. "I only saw him in the woods, and we nodded to each other, as hunters would do. But, I do think that the long-ear mule I saw is Fox's. It is strange that we had not seen it before."

"Maybe not," said Sees Beyond thoughtfully. "But, I am made to think that this is important."

"In what way?" asked Fox.

"I don't know," mused the holy woman. "Only, that it is. Some things, we must wait to learn what their meaning is."

"That is true," agreed Heron. "When Sees has this sort of feeling, I have learned not to question it."

"But where do we stand now on the trade?" asked Fox impatiently.

"We are considering," said Heron. "I think there are no other serious traders. They only want us to think so."

"Then that is good," said Fox.

"Yes, but when there is no reason to be urgent about it, it slows everything."

"I know," snapped Fox. He was becoming impatient, and I could truly understand that. I was too.

"When do they expect you back?" asked Fox.

Yes, of course. It was such a simple thing... I should have asked already. Would I ever grow to be as clever as even any one of these three adults with whom I was pushed into this situation? I felt that I had reason to doubt it. And this, too, came down hard on my mood. I was ready for something to happen.

Anything! I thought to myself. Anything to break this situation that was beginning to look so hopeless. It was a very stupid thought, at best.

Heron shrugged. "Nothing was said," he answered. "But I am made to think that they expect some sort of an offer, maybe tomorrow."

Sees Beyond nodded, without comment. But, there was a feeling on the part of all of us, though it was not spoken. The coming day would bring this torture to an end, one way or another.

I need to pause a little while now to explain about the things that happened next. As we all know, our People live in the grassland. We have, since Creation, some say. We move around, hunting, moving when the grass is scarce, grazed down by buffalo and by our own horses. Our holy men decide when to move, and in what direction.

At the end of a winter, the Holy Man decides when to burn the dry grass that is still standing. This is important, because to grow well, the grass must be grazed and must be burned, to keep it healthy. When this is done, the Sacred Hills become green again, and the buffalo return in answer to our prayers, dances, and ceremonies to bring them back. Yes, you know all of this. But it is a part of the Holy Man's gift, his way of looking across to the Other Side. Who of us has the gift to see when to burn? If our Holy Man guesses wrong, we would have a hungry year, no? Or we might burn our own camp! But this seldom happens. Our Holy Man knows, when the winds are right and the spirits are pleased, the best time to burn. Each season the burning is followed by the Sun Dance, to give thanks for the greening and the return of the buffalo to our tallgrass prairie, the Sacred Hills.

What I am trying to explain is that in the place where we were, this is not done. There are some places where the grass is taller and there are open spaces with a few trees. Nowhere, though, is there a big enough grassland place for a buffalo herd. Even a small one. Buffalo are not found there, except maybe a stray or two sometimes. So, no reason to burn. There are deer to hunt.

It seems to me, though, that the open grassland is where I belong...

Yes, forgive me. Yes, I am a son of the open prairie. I need to stretch my eyes to see the far edges of the world. How did I... Oh, yes, the burning... Without the fires each spring, to bring back the buffalo, the places where we were are grown up thickly with the pines and cedars, as well as oaks and other trees that I didn't even know their names.

I am made to think that all these trees, which break up the beauty of the grassland, the land of our buffalo, are there because the people who live there do not know about the spring burning. Among our People, it is a ceremony announced by our Holy Man, because he has the gift of knowing when the time is right. The burn brings back the sun, the grass, and the buffalo, on which our People depend. His medicine tells him when to burn.

What has this to do with my story? Let me go on. It is always an important ceremony, the burn. A light breeze is best, carrying the stripe of fire slowly across the open dry grass from last season. If the medicine is good, and the Holy Man has chosen his day well, and performs his prayer ritual sincerely, it will move across the plain in a line, raising a smoke as white as snow on the downwind side. It cleans the grassland, as a grooming brush and comb clean the winter fur from the skin of our horses. But, we all have seen, in an area where it has not been burned for a season or two, the damage that comes. Plants that are not part of the grassland come in... how, I do not know. Maybe the Holy Man knows. Maybe the seeds of trees and brush that will hurt the growth of the grass ride in, stuck to the fur or feathers of birds and animals.

They move north to south in the spring and fall, no? Maybe, just the wind...

Back to the burn. We have all seen what happens when the leading edge of the white-smoke finds a clearing that has not burned for a season or two. There will be brush and small trees, single plants such as the cedars and pines. What happens? When the fire reaches each small cedar tree, it will explode in a puff of black smoke and dark red flames, almost like the flash of fire that shoots the gun of the white man when it reaches the gunpowder.

This cleans the grassland and prepares it for a new grazing season. In the area where we were, they do not know of this, so they fail to burn, and they have no buffalo. And yes, this is important to my story! You will see!

CHAPTER THIRTY-SIX

Sees Beyond seemed to think that there were not really others interested in trading for White Plume.

"They are trying to make us think so," she told us. "That might make the price higher."

Such talk ripped at my heart. I knew that Sees Beyond was aware of this. But I also realized that this was her way to keep me alert. It would not be fair to me, for her to keep telling me "It will be all right," when it was not certain at all that this would come to a happy reunion. It would be dishonest for the holy woman to let me believe such a thing. Only when she could foresee what was coming could she show any real hope to Fox and to me.

I was, by then, beginning to feel a little "crazy" as the white man might say. One whose spirit becomes so restless that at any moment it might attempt to break free. It is not a pretty thing when such madness takes over a person's spirit.

We were in a very uncomfortable situation. There are only a few ways in which a young captive woman might be freed. She could be bought, traded for, freed by force, or by trickery. Any or all of these might be included in the efforts of Sees Beyond.

I had not realized that I could not be included in any of these methods. This did little to help my mood. If only there was some way to let White Plume know that help was coming. But Sees Beyond had been firm on that. There was too much risk if White Plume was aware that her father and I were near.

So, I spent another night with very little sleep, waking frequently from the throes of unspeakable dreams, in which...aahh... But never mind.

It was near morning when I woke, and lay watching the stars against the blackness that always seems to make the pre-dawn sky the darkest. I don't know what had wakened me. I rose and moved to the place we had chosen to empty our bladders. Maybe the full bladder was what had wakened me, but thinking back, probably not. There was a smell of smoke, which called my attention to our fire. No, the hardwood sticks had finished their smoking, and the glowing embers would have been good to cook with now. Maybe a stick or two, to keep the fire alive...

I rose and stepped to the wood pile, picking up three dry sticks, which I placed carefully on the hot coals. Among our people, as you know, three sticks of firewood, of three different woods, is best for a good fire. They burn at different speeds, some fast and bright, like willow, some slow but with a great heat, making hot coals to last all night, such as oak or other nut-trees.

I hurried back to my blankets and lay looking up at the sky. By this time there was the hint of a coming morning in the east. Not really light, but maybe just a paleness of the start against the dark sky, which now was graying along Earth's rim. There was the faint smell of smoke from the campfire as I settled back into my bed. Fox's soft snores told that he was having better luck at sleep than I was. I glanced at the Realstar in the north, the one that never moves. What would happen if it did, I wondered.

The air was still, except for a little stirring from the southwest, from time to time. Kookooskoos, the owl, called in the distance. I wondered if I could return to sleep now, as the morning sky continued to pale. The shifting breeze carried a puff of smoke from the fire...

But wait... There was something wrong about that smoke. It carried the scent of cedar... Leaves of cedar. I sat up, puzzled. I had put no green cedar on our fire, of course. Even whites would know that that would ruin anything cooked over such a fire. Well-seasoned cedar might serve for heat, but not for cooking.

Yet, I still smelled the cedar smoke, and now it seemed even stronger than before. Something was wrong, and badly so. The breeze from the southwest was picking up now, and the smell was becoming stronger.

Later, I was ashamed to realize that I should have been able to know what was happening. The direction of the wind, the unfamiliar smell of the burning of green cedar leaves... Oh, well... There was too much for my mind to handle just then, or I might have known, sooner.

About then, I heard again the cry of the owl, which may have had no real meaning. Except, that at the time, it seemed so. Who is to say? There is much about the spirit world... Yes, forgive me. I will go on.

Another twist of the wind, and I finally was made to know... A cedar, somewhere, was burning, and the light wind was carrying the scent toward us.

Even then, it was a little while before I saw that this could be a very dangerous thing. If the wind rose with the sun, as it often does, we could all be in the greatest danger of our lives.

CHAPTER THIRTY-SEVEN

I hurried to waken Fox, and as I did so, I began to see some things that I should have noticed before.

I had watched the sky as it paled in the east, but I now saw that a dawning was also to be seen in the southwest. The wind was rising, as if it had wakened with the dawn. It seemed to gain speed, fanning the fire with its own strength as it joined the twisting smoke.

A quick look told that the home of Sees Beyond and Heron would not be in much danger. Even in this situation, it could be seen that they had built wisely. Our camp, too, was well planned. Fox was experienced as a trader, and had learned many things in many different places. Far more, probably, than most men of his age.

But the two men who held White Plume captive had not been very wise in their camp. They were whites, of course. Some whites have been quick to learn our ways, but these were not ones whose wisdom could be counted on for a placement of their camp. Or, for anything else. It is hard to understand such persons, which again, makes them more dangerous. Which way would they go, what would they do in this very bad situation?

It was growing lighter. An owl soared past, heading away from the direction of the fire, adding wing-beats to hurry the retreat. A deer crashed through a patch of brush, across the open clearing, followed by a smaller one. Probably a doe and her fawn from the past autumn. Then another... Deer had been hunted heavily, but these had found deep woods or somewhere they could hide. Now, there was no place to offer shelter.

We heard yells of alarm now, mixed with a strange roaring sound at a distance upwind. Now, it could be seen that smoke and occasional glowing sparks were beginning to float across the clearings.

I could stand it no longer. I took foot at a dead run, toward where I knew the camp of the men who held White Plume stood. Fox yelled after me, but I kept running. I could not stand the danger to the woman I loved any longer...

The lightening of the dawn was making it easier to see the smoke, drifting downwind across the open spaces. It was also becoming heavy enough to cause a burning in my lungs and watering of my eyes. A heavy layer of smoke lay ahead, and I was trying to decide... run around the heaviest smoke, or try to stay low, beneath most of it? Fox was yelling... I glanced back and could not see him. I rushed ahead, no longer sure of direction. Everything had taken on a different appearance.

A figure moved ahead of me in the foggy smoke. Another deer... no! A mule, tied to a tree... It was fighting and frantically pulling on the rope that held it, almost in a panic. Even in this situation, the thing to do would be to loose the animal. I hurried over and began to struggle with the rope as the mule's pulling tightened it. I needed some slack to untie it, and the constant pull prevented such a move. It would have been easy to panic, and I nearly did so. I was not sure why I found myself trying to free someone else's mule. It simply seemed to be the thing to do. I was nearly ready to leave the mule to his fate and move on, when I saw movement from another figure, beyond the animal. A man, only dimly seen through the floating smoke and in the uneven light of the coming dawn. It was plain that he saw me. It was one of the hairy-faced ones.

What now? We were all in danger, especially the mule, because he was tied and could not run from the flames. If there was time, I might have cut the rope, or calmed the mule enough to untie it. A horse, by this time, might have completely panicked.

There was more than one problem here... The hair-face seemed more occupied with me than with the mule, who was still fighting the rope. The man stepped around the mule and the tree, and moved toward me. I had no weapon, and the other man carried a small axe. He might throw it, or just hack with it. Neither idea looked very good from my position. If only... I was still thinking of my chances if I would simply turn and run. But then, a thrown axe...

I dodged around, trying to keep the mule between us as the other man circled to gain a chance to use his axe.

Then a desperate idea struck me. I was now certain that the animal was, in fact, Fox's stolen mule. Its manners, its stance, everything about it began to seem familiar. It was still pulling back on the rope, but I now recalled the habit that I had seen once when White Plume's brother had been teasing the animal. Maybe...

I circled, dodging away from the hair-face with the axe, keeping the mule between us. A little farther... Now! The man with the axe was circling now straight behind the mule. I was at the animal's flank... I dug a thumb into the soft spot just ahead of the hip. I had seen White Plume's brother do this, and had been disgusted with him, but now...

The mule lashed out with both feet, just as the hair-face moved into position. One hind foot struck his shoulder, a glancing blow, but the other... Aiee! The hoof landed squarely in the man's face. He was thrown backward, and landed limply on his back, his nose and mouth a bloody pulp. His body jerked a little and lay quiet. I had no idea whether he was alive or dead, but he was surely out of action.

I leaned over just as Fox came running. He paused to view the scene, and let out a long breath.

"*Aiee!*"

CHAPTER THIRTY-EIGHT

It took only a moment for both of us to understand the situation. We now had a real advantage, in any contact with White Plume's remaining captor. Our problem was not with him, but with the fire. We, ourselves, were in great danger, and, what about White Plume?

Fox stepped forward and picked up the axe. With one stroke he cut the rope from around the tree. As it went slack, the mule bolted away, quickly disappearing in the thickening smoke.

I started to run in the direction that I felt was to lead us into the camp of White Plume's captors.

"No, this way!" called Fox.

I turned to follow him, and in the space of a few heartbeats, we ran into a heavy and solid growth of cedar brush. Somehow, in the dense smoke and the twisting and changing wind, we had become unsure of direction.

It was growing lighter, which was really no help. The sun's rays on the curls of smoke was no help, either. The shifting wind seemed to make the directions change, without warning.

"This way!" called Fox.

I would have gone in another direction, but followed Fox. In only a heartbeat or two he had run headlong into the trunk of a large cottonwood tree.

I thought I heard a woman's voice, crying out in alarm. Who could it be, but White Plume? I dodged around the cottonwood tree and hurried toward the cry, choking and coughing the smoke as I ran. I could see two figures ahead, struggling and pushing. I turned in that direction.

One, as could be expected, was a hair-faced white man. I had no way of knowing whether it was one of the men holding White Plume captive. I had never seen either of them at a close distance. Besides, as we have said before, whites all look pretty much alike, no?

The other person, of course, was White Plume. I would have recognized her from the proud way she carried herself, tall and strong, and the way she moved, with dignity and purpose.

I rushed toward them, with no better weapon than the knife at my waist. There was no time to even wish that I had the axe that Fox still carried. I glanced back, but in the shifting smoke I could not even see him. He may have gone in some other direction, I thought.

I started toward the struggling pair, stumbling through the brushy growth. Of course, there was a path somewhere, but I had never seen it. I was completely at a loss, even as to where to look for a path. My eyes were stinging and watering badly, and I began to cough from the smoke. Just then, the smoke parted for a moment and I caught a better glimpse at the struggling pair. The man was trying to grab White Plume's wrist, while she kept grabbing for the knife at his waist. He swung a heavy fist to her head, as white men do when they fight, and White Plume stumbled backward. The man still held her wrist, with his other hand, and raised his fist to strike again.

I was still too far away to be of any help, but White Plume moved as quickly and as smoothly as a snake strikes... In one sweeping move of her free hand she grabbed the weapon at the man's waist. Without even a pause in the sweep, her motion circled the two struggling persons. The knife struck, White Plume pulled away, and left the hilt sticking out from the soft underbelly of the paleface. He stared at it for the space of a few heartbeats and his eyes seemed to go blank as he sank limply to the ground.

White Plume stepped quickly to retrieve the knife, and turned toward us, ready to fight. In the uncertain light, it took her a moment to see what was happening. Of course, she had no idea that we were anywhere near at all.

Surely, it must have been a complete surprise to see either of us in this way. She had no way to know that we were in the area, unless Sees Beyond and Heron had been able to inform her. That seemed unlikely, and they had not mentioned it.

White Plume stood, still ready to fight, the knife in her hand pointed in our direction.

"White Plume..." said her father cautiously.

It must have been a hard thing for her to understand, after the long time she had been captive.

"Father... " She still held the knife in a defensive way, not quite ready to believe what was happening. She looked toward me.

"Badger?"

I wanted to run toward her, but it would be foolish. One should not run toward a somewhat confused woman who had just killed her captor, and stood with the knife ready to use again.

But, the next few moments became even more confusing. As we stood, all three hardly able to believe what was happening, I saw White Plume's eyes lift to look at something which seemed to be behind us.

"Look out!" she cried.

I whirled to see what had startled her, and had not completely turned when something struck me from behind, just below my right knee. I did not even see it coming. A heavy club... out of nowhere, it seemed. I fell heavily. I had never felt such pain.

Fox stepped past me and quickly struck down my attacker. But who could it be? It took a little while to recognize the bloody-faced victim of the mule's kick. He had fallen so heavily that there had seemed no doubt that his skull was crushed. I had completely forgotten him, until now. And now, it was over.

Not completely over, of course, but the wind seemed not blowing with the strength that it had been. There was a change in the sort of danger we had faced, and were still facing.

But, we had recovered Fox's daughter, who meant the world to me. We could start back, to rejoin the People.

But before that, even, we needed to see how the holy couple who had been such a great help to us had fared in the fire.

Fox made me as comfortable as he could, and left me with White Plume while he went to the house of Heron and Sees Beyond.

Their house had been spared. Fox told how it appeared that the fire had split, and passed around their lodge, with very little damage.

The holy couple, who had become such a powerful part of our lives, now seemed much like ordinary people. White Plume had gained much help from Sees. As the bargaining went on, the holy woman had managed to let her know that help was near. Truly, their medicine is powerful, and must have been guiding our experiences all along.

It took a few days to rejoin the trader's family, and to start back toward my own. It was not a simple thing, of course. We were not ready, in preparation and planning, to start to travel. We had had no warning that one of us would be forced to travel on a travois. It was slow and painful. A travois does not make a good bed. I have new respect for those who must travel that way.

My family came searching for me, we met and started back to the Sun Dance.

What? The trader and his family? Yes, they will join us later. Fox must stock his trade goods for the season. I have learned much about the life of a trader's family. He has asked me to partner. Maybe I will do that... My leg heals well, but maybe not well enough to ride in the hunts. We will see...

అఖ

The Buckskin Calendar (in the pictographic history of the People) from that year suggests that the young couple did marry, with the husband becoming a partner to his wife's father, a respected trader. It is said that he always walked with a slight limp...

Some have asked more about the holy couple, who so strongly influenced the lives of Badger and White Plume and their families. There were more questions about a holy man who could change himself into a bird, and could create happenings beyond all understanding. No one ever saw him make such medicine. His wife, Sees Beyond, a holy woman herself, must have had very powerful medicine, too. Perhaps, even more than that of Heron.

It has been noted that in the pictograph which seems to represent Badger and White Plume, the background of the sky appears to be aflame, or to represent a sunset. There is also represented what seems to be a large bird, such as an eagle or perhaps a heron, soaring over a landscape with heavy timber, rather than the traditional grassland of the People... We must make our own interpretation.

Moon of Madness

AFTER-WORDS

My Indian friends tell me, only half joking, "Don't get any closer to modern times! Nothing good will be happening."

That's about right.

I expect to continue with historical fiction and non-fiction as well as short stories, many including Indian characters.

Originally, I did not intend to write from the Indian point of view. Actually, I fought it a little. (I use the term "Indian," rather than "Native American," which is a government-issue label, because my friends use "Indian.")

It has been an honor to be accepted, often without seeking this acceptance. Sometimes, while signing books, I have been asked by readers, obviously native, "What is your own tribe?"

That, to me, may be the greatest honor of all. My background is German and Scottish, but I am frequently told that "You have a very powerful guide."

I see no conflict in this with my own religious beliefs. I have found no case among any of the hundreds of American Indian cultures, in which anyone was ever killed over religion. For other reasons, maybe, but not religious belief. "You have yours, I have mine. We do not challenge what God said to you."

Christians, on the other hand, have historically killed other Christians over differences about Christianity. They still do so. Is something wrong with the picture, here?

I must admit, I've taught a Christian Sunday School class for many years, but have tried to use the tolerance for other interpretations that I have learned from my "Native" friends.

There is a story among the Kiowas about a visit from a Christian priest, very early in their contact with whites. The Kiowa "holy man," in an appropriate response to the priest's story, began to narrate their story of God, the Creator.

The priest was greatly offended, and scolded them for "worshiping the wrong God!"

This, of course, was equally offensive to the Kiowas. It should have been an informative exchange of ideas. The Kiowa holy man tried to smooth things over, using the Indian term of respect, "Uncle."

"We apologize, Uncle. We did not know that there is more than one God."

And Christians kill Christians today.

CPSIA information can be obtained at www.ICGtesting.com
Printed in the USA
LVOW06*0059220815

451136LV00003B/15/P